Crime and Punishment
in Derbyshire

© Peter J Naylor, 2010

All Rights Reserved. No part of this publication may be reproduced, stored in a retrieval system, or transmitted in any form or by any means – electronic, mechanical, photocopying, recording, or otherwise – without prior written permission from the publisher

Published by Sigma Leisure – an imprint of
Sigma Press, Stobart House, Pontyclerc, Penybanc Road
Ammanford, Carmarthenshire SA18 3HP

British Library Cataloguing in Publication Data

A CIP record for this book is available from the British Library

ISBN: 978-1-85058-866-5

Typesetting and Design by: Sigma Press, Ammanford, Wales

Photographs: © Peter J Naylor (unless otherwise stated)

Cover photographs:

Printed by: Bell & Bain Limited, Glasgow

Every effort has been made to fulfil requirements with regard to reproducing copyright material. The author and publisher will be glad to rectify any ommissions at the earliest opportunity.

Disclaimer: The information in this book is given in good faith and is believed to be correct at the time of publication.

Crime and Punishment in Derbyshire

over the centuries

Peter J Naylor

I dedicate this book to my wife Marian and my son Jonathan

Contents

Introduction	9
Highwaymen and Footpads	17
Dick Turpin	17
Inns and Public Houses	18
Lantern Pike	19
The Winnats	20
Cutthroat Bridge	21
Bold Nevison	21
John Waltyre	22
Moon Inn, Stoney Middleton	22
Black Harry	23
A rogue and vagabond	23
Footpads at Derby	24
Domestic Strife	26
Unhappy Christmas	26
Poison at Rushton Spencer	26
Coal Pit murders	27
Buried alive	31
Passion	33
George Fox	33
Murder at the Grange	33
The Padley Martyrs	37
A duel at Winster	38
Murder on a boat	39
The tragedy of Joan Waste	40
A poisoning	40
A horrible murder at Agard Street	41
Ronald Smedley	43
Daylight robbery	46
They hang 'em in bunches at Heage	46
The Magpie Mine murders	49
The Coterol Gang	49

George Woodcock — 51
The confessions of Percival Cooke and James Tomlinson — 53
The theft of £400 — 53
Charlie Peace — 54
A brave policeman — 58

Revolution and mayhem — 59
The Pentrich Revolution — 59
Reform Act riots — 61
The Battle of Piesefield — 64
Prize fight — 64

High Treason and assassination — 66
Anthony Babington — 66
The Phoenix Park murders, Dublin — 67

Murder — 69
Murder in the frankpledge of Bontesol — 69
Murder in a church — 69
The Bakewell 'Tart' — 70
Pottery Cottage — 72
The copy-cat murders — 73
'A Horrid and Inhuman Murder' — 74
'A Bloody and Inhuman Murder' — 75
Enoch Stone — 77
Samuel Marshall of Repton — 80
The rag and bone man — 81
Bones in a cesspit — 83
Jealousy — 85

Suicide, patricide, matricide and infanticide — 87
Suicide — 87
  Mather's grave — 87
  A curious poisoning at the Snake Inn — 88
  Attempted suicide and murder — 89
Abortions and Infanticide — 89
  A woman in the Pillory — 89
  Mary Spencer — 90
  Common in Derby — 91

Patricide	91
The water cure	91
George Hobbs o	93
Ilkeston parracide	95
Matricide	96
Mary Fallon of Chesterfield	96
Ada Knighton of Ilkeston	98

A miscellany

	100
Prostitution	100
Matlock to London	100
Alice Newsome	100
The Resurrectionists	101
The Monocled Mutineer	102
Poaching	106
Hung for a sheep	107
Sheep Stealing	107
Hung twice	109
Sheep stealing at Calow	109
Bestiality	110
Pressing to death	110
Arson	111
Mass Trespass	111
Bigamy	114
Eleven wives	114
Wife selling	115
Gambling	116
Road Traffic Offences	116
A load of timber in Glossop	117
Witchcraft	117

Sources and acknowledgements	119
About the author	121

Introduction

Crime fascinates us all, particularly murders, and the bloodier they are the better they are received. However, whilst this book gives much of its space over to murder, other crimes are also included. The details of the court cases have been excluded as they can be both boring and tedious for the reader.

This book is about crime within the County of Derbyshire. It would appear that the Peak District was a unruly place until recently, mainly due to poor roads, lawlessness, being sparsely populated and dark by night. Travellers had little choice when it came to travelling across the area to get from east to west and north to south or vice versa. An ideal scenario for robbers.

Highway robbery became popular during the civil war of the 17th Century, when many who took the side of the King were cast out to fend for themselves. When the monarchy was restored they had already committed crimes for which they could hang and were unable to pursue an honourable career.

Derby Gaol

This history uses many murders as subject matter due to their being well recorded in newspapers and legend. Lesser crimes attracted less attention. The following list explains their nature. There is much misconception about their meanings. Starting with the worst first:

Burnt to death

This was reserved for religious heretics but having said that the only such punishment in the County of Derby was the death of Joan Waste in 1601. She adopted the Church of England in the face of Catholic opposition. Traditionally the executioner usually strangled the victim before the flames reached the victim. Even so, this punishment was excessive even by the standards of the time. See Chapter 4, 'The tragedy of Joan Waste'. Thankfully this was a rare punishment, it was most popular in the 16th century especially under Mary I and Elizabeth I on religious grounds.

Hanging, drawing and quartering

This hideous penalty was for treason only. This most gruesome and cruel punishment was carried out as follows: the victim was dragged on a hurdle pulled by a horse from the prison to the execution site. The official sentence was, 'You shall be hanged by the neck and being alive cut down, your privy members shall be cut off and your bowels taken out and burned before you, your head severed from your body and your body divided into four quarters to be disposed of at the King's (Queen's) pleasure'. One cannot imagine the pain and anguish this caused the victim, death must have come as a relief. This was first instigated by Edward Longshanks and was used for five hundred years to our eternal shame. It surpassed in barbarity any other punishment known to man at that time.

The last time this punishment was handed out was in Derby (see Chapter 6, 'The Pentrich Revolution').

Hanging

We are all familiar with this sentence, now long since abolished in this country it remained on the statute book for certain other offences until 1998. It is still the preferred method in other countries including certain states in the USA.

We are all familiar with the Judge's sentence 'You will be taken to a place of execution where you will be hanged until you are dead, and may God have mercy on your soul'.

Hanging originally was to suspend the victim from a gallows, sometimes a tree, with a rope round his neck which was then raised until

Introduction

St Webburgh's Church where the hanged were ofton buried

his feet were off the ground. This meant that he would choke to death with his limbs twitching. It is on record that a man hung like this for eight hours before dying.

Hanging sometimes appeared as a shambles years ago. A notable instance was the hanging of four men for arson at North Wingfield. They commenced singing a hymn when a shower of rain descended upon them whereupon two of them took shelter under an umbrella held over the drop and a third one retreated to a doorway for shelter. A man who had murdered someone at Barlborough was to be hung and as he was hanged the rope slipped to the ground; the executioner had to resort to tying the criminal up again. The surgeons took his body for dissecting. Finally, a burglar went to his execution in a mourning coach followed by a hearse. He helped the executioner to secure the rope to a tree, he then pulled the cap over his head and threw himself from the coach to hang.

County Court and Gaol

If these events had not been so serious they could have been an entertainment to those watching. What is obvious is that so many went to their deaths willingly and sometimes in good humour. Many of these were plied with alcohol by the then governor of the Derby Gaol who doubled his salary this way. The number of hangings were many and clearly did not act as a deterrent from crime. The sixty years following 1770 were known as the Bloody Code as it appeared that one could be hanged for almost any offence, even trivial ones such as stealing three pennies. To add to the drama Javelin Men were in attendance at most hangings of the 18th century and beyond. As the name implies they carried a javelin each as a symbol of their authority as a member of a Sheriff's retinue and/or a Judge's escort to the assizes. Judging by the illustrations which have survived of these men, it seems that they carried anything from a pike to a spear.

Old Police Station at Wirksworth

The last judicial hanging was of Edward Slack in Derby on 16 July, 1907; the last at Derby Gaol was Cotton in 1898. The first to suffer the short drop were Cooke and Tomlinson (see Chapter 5, 'The Confessions of Percival Cooke and James Tomlinson').

The first recorded public hangings were of six people in 1341. The last public hanging in Derby was of Richard Thorley for murdering Eliza Morrow in 1819. Perhaps the youngest to be hanged was Hannah Docking who had poisoned another girl, also in 1819.

This gave way by the 19th century to dropping the victim by removing the place on which he stood or sat. A longer rope was used with the intention of breaking his neck. This was made 'more human' by the invention of the drop, whereby the prisoner stood on a hinged flap, which was opened so that the victim was in free fall for a distance before the rope broke his neck. There were many executioners who failed in their duty causing the slow strangulation of the victim until the executioner pulled on his legs to speed matters up. A recent executioner was the

Introduction

House of Correction at Wirksworth

famous Albert Pierrepoint of Manchester who devised a table which gave the length of the drop based on the victim's neck structure, height and weight.

Almost all Derbyshire hangings took place in front of the County Court on Saint Mary's Gate, Derby and town hangings in front of the Derby Gaol on Vernon Street. Most of the bodies were buried in quick lime within the confines of the prisons, a good number were buried in the churchyard of Saint Werburgh's in Derby and many were used for teaching anatomy to medical students. The abolition of the death penalty was slow in getting through Parliament. The Death Penalty Acts of 1965 and 1968 put an end to capital punishment, except for treason and piracy with violence, first enacted in 1351 and last used in 1946. Now that the UK is a member of the European Community the death penalty has been abolished.

Hanging Bridge at Ashbourne crosses the River Dove and goes into Mayfield, Staffordshire, which has a road named Gallowstree Lane. Any connection with capital punishment cannot be found.

Flogging and Birching

Flogging was administered to the victim's bare back, usually until the blood flowed freely or a set number of lashes had been administered. This was more common in the armed forces, especially the Royal Navy. A penalty of 500 lashes are on record causing certain death to the victim. It is also on record that such severe punishments exposed the victim's kidneys.

Birching, still used within living memory, was to deliver a set number of strokes using a bundle of birch twigs on a bare back. This was a favourite punishment for young offenders, normally youths. A doctor was always in attendance for removing pieces of twig from the wounds of the

County Gaol with new drop. Note the Javelin Men

victim as well as ensuring that he did not die. These penalties would have been undertaken either in private or in public.

It is on record that, in 1735 at Bakewell, two women were flogged bare breasted in public. In 1791 the flogging of women was banned.

Prison
The confinement to a prison is the oldest punishment on record. This in itself is a vast topic and space does not permit addressing it here. The prisons which served Derbyshire were located in Derby. These were:

> Cornmarket, 1652 - 1750s
>
> Friar Gate, 1756 - 1846, where the cells still exist and are open to the public
>
> Vernon Street, 1843 - 1929, where the facade exists, commonly known as the Derby Gaol
>
> Saint Mary's Gate for the County of Derby still serves as a court of law

Gibbet
The gibbet was usually administered after the death of the victim, however a few were gibbeted alive. The bodies of the dead were gibbeted were often coated with tar to ensure their preservation for as long as possible. Either way the birds had their feast. The gibbet was usually an iron cage but sometimes chains were used. This device was normally erected at a cross roads for all to see. Those who were gibbeted alive died of exposure and starvation.

Lingard was gibbeted and his body slowly rotted and was scavenged by crows for eleven years, after which it was taken down and the skull exhibited at Belle View, a popular centre of entertainment in Manchester.

Stocks
We are all familiar with the stocks – a device for securing minor offenders, leaving their hands and faces or feet as targets for any rubbish the public may desire to throw at the captive. Original examples can be seen at Eyam and Sudbury.

Transportation
When Britain's colonies were new and needed able people to work on these barren lands, many, mostly male, miscreants were sentenced to

deportation for periods from four years to life. If they survived their sentences to the full they had to find their own fare home. Many of these men significantly helped in the foundation of Australia. This is also addressed in Chapter 6 – 'The Pentrich Revolution'.

Other punishments

Without going into detail, there were other village punishments such as scolds bridles, ducking stools, etc. References to these punishments are not evident in Derbyshire, probably because they were a village affair outside the scope of the law. It is pertinent to note that the use of such punishments were directed at women mostly and rarely to the men!

Footnote

Nearly all the crimes mentioned in this book occur today but with much more lenient sentences.

Highwaymen and Footpads

Dick Turpin

Of all the criminals in the past this man is best remembered. Some look upon him as a heroic man who acted as a latter day Robin Hood. He was nothing of the sort. His famous ride from London to York is often quoted; the feat was not possible unless he could have ridden his horse at 13 miles per hour without stopping for food, water and sleep for both. If he had stayed at every house, hostelry and inn as claimed by the various occupiers he would have had to live well over a hundred years.

He was a bad lot from his youth and until his death. He learned early of the means of getting rich quickly. His father was a party to Dick's pursuits and being an inn keeper he was also a smuggler. Dick was born at Hempstead, near Mildenhall in Essex and was apprenticed to a butcher in Whitechapel, London. This was followed by his marriage to Elizabeth Millington in 1728; there is no record of any children being born. At this time it would appear that he started his own business as a butcher but found that buying the animals was pointless, it was much cheaper to steal them. This was his first lawless venture. He was caught stealing two animals but he managed to escape and he then became an outlaw.

He joined the Gregory Gang who were active in the South of England. They specialised in robbing remote dwellings and farms, poaching deer and other larger animals, including horses. At one house they raided Turpin threatened to roast an old lady alive if she refused to divulge where she hid her money. Eventually the gang holed themselves up in an inn in London but Turpin escaped through a window and ran off. In 1737, he had a price of £100 on his head for his capture, a considerable sum in those days.

Now alone, he decided together with Captain Tom King to pursue highway robbery. The term captain was of course false, but King did establish an element of fair play into his exploits and this might be why Turpin was also given some sympathy. It could be that Turpin's reputation was borrowed from King. The truth about Turpin was much more scandalous as he had already killed to avoid arrest and accidentally shot to death his partner. Or was it an accident? King, before he died told the authorities about Turpin's deeds, hideouts and friends. This is when Turpin supposedly rode his famous horse, Black Bess, from Essex to York.

On arrival in York he took on the name of John Palmer, Gentleman. This latter was accorded to men who did not have to work to make a living. He set up as a stock dealer but stealing was again more profitable. The Turpin of old was back in business again.

One day when in his cups, he shot an inn keeper's game cock. He was arrested and the authorities learned about his pursuits. To seal his fate, Turpin wrote to his brother-in-law at Hempstead, which letter was examined by his old school teacher who recognised his hand writing. From now on Turpin was a doomed man.

On the 7th April, 1739, he was taken to the York Gallows on Knavesmire, now covered by the race course. He was a jack-my-lad even on this occasion. He was dressed in a new outfit, waved to the crowd as the cart carried him from York and addressed the spectators for half an hour. The hangman was Thomas Hadfield, who for a pardon had given the authorities a full confession of the crimes the gang had committed in return for his life. Finally, Turpin cheated the hangman by throwing himself off the scaffold without breaking his neck. He died five minutes later, aged 32. Robbers disinterred Turpin's corpse for selling to anatomists but this scheme went wrong and he was buried in Saint George's Church graveyard, York.

We have little concrete evidence of Turpin in Derbyshire. When in York he raided south to Lincolnshire, Nottinghamshire and Derbyshire. There are numerous claims of inns and dwellings which were visited by Turpin, including the Turpin Lead Mine at Bonsall Moor, near Matlock and the Owl Coaching Inn, Blackbrook, near Belper, now a private residence.

The Peacock Inn at Oakerthorpe near Alfreton, has been a stopping place for travellers over the centuries. A horseshoe found in the cellar was reputed to have been shed by Black Bess when vaulting a toll bar, en route to York. The innkeeper at this time must have made a fortune by letting the gullible handle the shoe when quaffing their pints.

Just north of this establishment is Higham on the same turnpike, where a cottage owner was led to believe that Turpin spent a night here.

Holly Bush Inn at Makeney, south of Milford was reputedly a stop-over for Turpin. It is located on the old turnpike road from Derby to York. In the 18th century a pair of pistols were found hidden in a wall – by Turpin?

Inns and Public Houses
Until Victorian times such establishments in the depths of the countryside were easy targets for robbers. Highwaymen originated after our Civil War

Highwaymen and Footpads　　　　　　　　　　　　　　　　　　　　　19

of the 17th Century when many royalist soldiers found themselves destitute. However the expression highwayman was known before this war.

Lantern Pike

Lantern Pike is a hill close to the A624, the Glossop to Chapel en le Frith road. At Little Hayfield is the Lantern Inn, known at the time of this story as the New Inn. On 11th November 1927 a regular customer, Amos Dawson, had arrived at the inn to find it locked, so he waited at the door for the publican's husband. It was 6 o'clock early evening and the inn was usually open well before this time. Amy Collinson kept the inn whilst her husband worked elsewhere, a common arrangement with country inns at this time. The husband along with Amos forced an entry to find Amy dead with much blood about her. On examination both men found a wound in her neck with a knife embedded in it. She also had other damage which suggested that the murderer had struck her as she fell. However, the two concluded that she had taken her own life.

The police arrived in the form of two officers; Assistant Chief Constable James Garrow with the Head of the CID, Walter Else. They examined the body and concluded quickly that they were looking for a murderer and robber, as it was found that the float in the till totalling

Lantern Inn, Upper Hayfield

£40 was missing. The hunt was on! They interviewed the regular attendees at the inn, and the officers quickly suspected George Frederick Walter Hayward, alias Gerry. Gerry was unemployed and drew the dole, which meant that he had to go to New Mills to collect it.

The police had two witnesses who remember Gerry behaving oddly on the morning of the murder; Tommy Barr had seen Gerry walking towards New Mills dressed in a large black mackintosh, which seemed unsuitable as it was a dry day. A neighbour, Maud Lillian McBain aged 13 had witnessed Gerry cutting a lead waste pipe from the sink at his house. It was later learned that this was the cosh used against Amy. It was later found hidden in a water cistern at the New Inn. There were blood stains on his hat which matched the victim's blood group. When searching his house the police found money hidden in the chimney and the murderer stated that it was money which he owed his last employer.

He was tried at the Derby Assizes in February, 1928. Soon after the trial started a juryman collapsed and a new jury had to be sworn in, who found him guilty as charged. Hayward was hanged by Thomas Pierrepoint, uncle of the famous Albert.

The Winnats

The Winnats (from the old English 'the gate or portal of the wind') is a steep and rocky slope west of Castleton and at the time of this tale was a turnpike road.

In 1768, a young couple, Allen (or Henry?) and Clara were making their way to the Peak Forest Chapel, which was 'Extra-Parochial' and marriages could be performed there with little notice. Another such was the Parish Church of South Wingfield, Derbyshire and Gretna Green in Scotland is similar.

After a long and tiring day they found themselves taking refreshment at an inn in the village whilst being watched by a group of lead miners. On their way up the Winnats the couple were waylaid, dragged to a barn and were murdered; Allen by means of his throat being cut and Clara by a pick-axe. It must have been a bloody affair. Their bodies were buried in the floor of the barn. Their horses were found at Sparrowpit and taken with the saddles to Chatsworth but were never claimed. One of the saddles can be seen at the shop outside Speedwell Cavern at the foot of the Winnats.

The culprits were never arrested but they seemingly paid a price for their crime: one broke his neck in the Winnats; another was crushed under a fall of stone; a third took his own life; the fourth became insane. Only the last man died in comfort and made a death bed confession.

Ten years after the event the bodies of the young couple were found buried in the barn.

Several people have tried to piece together the 'true' tale and this seems to be the most popular version of the story.

Cutthroat Bridge

This small stone built bridge is close to Ladybower Reservoir and was named many years after the act that caused a murder at this lonely spot. Near to the turn of the 16th century this location was a ford for packhorses in Highshaw (locally Earnshaw) Clough and around this time a Robert Ridge came across a man with a cut to his throat. In 1635 his deposition was placed on record, 'Found a man with a wound in his throat ... carried him to the house in Ladybower'.

The man was still alive and a group of men carried him to a farmhouse half a mile distant and then on to Bamford Hall where he died, two days after his discovery. The present bridge was built in 1812 by Thomas Telford when constructing a new road from Sheffield to Glossop. Much of this road is now the A57 and it was named Cuttthroat Bridge in memory of what happened there.

History nearly repeated itself later when a headless corpse was found near to the bridge. Two men from Sheffield were found guilty of this crime.

Bold Nevison

Also known as Swift Nick Nevison and John or William, he was active in the Hope Valley in the 1680s just before his death in 1684 aged approximately forty-four years. He was a latter day Robin Hood, robbing the rich and helping the poor. One incident does him much credit. Nevison came across a farmer from Padley who had sold some live stock at Bakewell Market. They shared a drink and rode towards the farmer's home. They arrived at Stoke when Nevison drew his pistol and demanded the money from the hapless farmer who begged to be allowed to keep his cash pleading that his family would be homeless, indeed his reason for selling the beasts was to pay the rent. All to no avail for Nevison rode off with his spoils.

During the night before rent day, the farmer heard two shots coming from the bridge at Grindleford nearby. He heard the hooves of a horse and one of his windows being broken. On investigation he found a bag of money equal in value to the rent owed plus a guinea (an old gold coin representing £1 1s or £1.05 today and still referred to in the names of some horse races. The gold was from a colony named New Guinea.)

Nevison was eventually caught and was hanged at York on 4th May, 1684.

John Waltyre

John was travelling by horse from Bakewell to Leek when he was caught in a thunder storm. He decided to spend the night in an ale house. On entering the inn, John saw some dubious looking men having a drink.

On entering his room for the night, he found a corpse in a cupboard. He decided to escape but found the window was barred. He decided to go to bed and brave it out until the next day when he laid his head down in a pool of blood. He braced the door with a chest to prevent it from being opened and broke a chair from which he took an arm to use as a weapon if the need should arise. He then spotted a trap door in the floor below the bed. He quickly moved the bed away from the trap door. Next, someone started to gain entry by turning the door handle. On enquiring from John as to what the stranger wanted he was told that he needed a blanket for another guest. John declared that there were none to spare.

The trap door started to be raised and lowered, then the door handle was rattled and John threatened to fire his pistol through the door if they persisted. Early next morning he descended the stairs to find the men asleep. He mounted his horse and fled with the men in pursuit.

John told this tale before he died in 1810. Fact or a good yarn? Possibly the latter!

Moon Inn, Stoney Middleton

The Moon Inn (originally the Man in the Moon Inn) still stands on the A623 Middleton to Chapel en le Frith road, close to Lovers' Leap on the edge of Stony Middleton. A pedlar from Scotland was killed by a group of local pedlars; the event was ignored by the publican. The females in the group took the pedlar's body on the back of a horse along the dale and deposited it in a well known cave called Carlswark Cavern.

This happened in August 1760 and on 2 June, 1763, his skeleton was discovered along with his shoes. The remains were placed in a box and deposited in Eyam church for some years and were eventually interred by the then incumbent, the Reverend Seward in the churchyard at the church. The bell ringer, Matthew Hall, was given the shoes which he wore out.

The name and circumstances of the unfortunate man was a mystery which has recently been unravelled due to some superb research by Roger Flindall. It appears that the man was a Scot named Campbell, a travelling dealer.

Highwaymen and Footpads

Moon Inn, Stoney Middleton

Black Harry
Little is known about this highwayman, except that he is commemorated by Black Harry Lane, from Moisty Lane and Middleton Lane which connects to Black Harry Gate, Stoney Middleton, a village that also boasts a house named after Harry.

He was very active on the upland above Great Longstone and Wardlow, by preying on the Jaggers who led the packhorses. He was caught and gibbeted at Wardlow Mires nearby. One can assume that this would have been a live gibbeting as a reference to hanging cannot be found, indeed we do not know the dates when he was active.

A rogue and vagabond
Rider, a young man in his early twenties was a weaver from Yorkshire. He joined a gang of pickpockets and fraudsters who practiced their art amongst large gatherings of the public such as at race meetings and fairs.

When at Buxton Races he was apprehended for dipping his hand into the pocket of a gentleman. He was taken to Tideswell House of Correction pending his trial at Chesterfield, where he was sent down to do three months of hard labour at the Derby House of Correction as a 'rogue and vagabond'.

When released he did not waste any time. He went North on the turnpike as far as Makeney. He attacked Mary Barton and stole six half-pennies and with this money he went to the nearest hostelry to buy a drink. He did not know that he had been followed by the toll-keeper who had heard Mary's cries. He chased Rider and apprehended him.

At the March Assizes he faced the charges of robbery and ravishment. The trial was a long one and he was indicted for robbery on the King's Highway. This being a capital offence it left the judge, Sir Nathan Grose, with no alternative but to sentence him to death. He was committed to Derby Gaol and was shackled in his cell.

He protested that he was drunk at the time he attacked Mary Barton and that he did not know what he was about. The Prison Chaplain tried to persuade Rider to repent and to make a full confession. He remained unrepentant. He did say that it was well that his career was coming to an end as it was likely that he would have gone back to his old ways.

He made an attempt to escape with the help of a light and a stone. He managed to free himself from his fetters and started to make a hole in the wall. The gaoler entered his cell and caught him at it.

Five days later on All Fools Day, 1791, he faced his execution in Derby. He made his last farewells and received the sacrament. On the arrival of the Under-Sheriff and the Javelin Men he was placed in a cart to be carried through the streets of Derby before a large turn-out of spectators. Following the customary prayers the cart was moved and he died at the end of a rope. A morality tale of what can happen when in the grip of the demon drink.

Footpads at Derby

In October, 1776, a Mr Ready Ledwith, an upholster in Derby, was returning home from a short ride on his horse when he was stopped on Osmaston Road by four footpads, one of whom held a pistol and another was armed with a long knife.

They pulled Ledwith off his horse and saluted him with a volley of terrifying oaths. Following this softening up procedure they robbed him of fourteen shillings (70p) but refused his watch which was of chased metal, probably made individually with a maker's name and its own serial number engraved on it. Thus it would have been highly incriminating when prosecuting were a thief in possession of such a watch.

Domestic Strife

Unhappy Christmas

Two witnesses, both lead miners, had seen Edward Wager kicking a woman and pushing her towards the Bleaklow Dam, one of several located in the lead workings. She shouted for help but the miners decided to keep out of the way and continued walking when they saw Wager returning to his home at Bleaklow Farm without his wife.

Another miner, William Goddard when walking home in the twilight, found Harriet Wager's body floating in the dam. He hurried to Stoney Middleton to seek Inspector Cruit and together they went to the dam where they recovered Harriet and carried her body to Bleaklow Farm. Wager swore that his wife had drowned herself due to her jealousy of a Alice Hancock. After spending the night in the Bakewell lock-up, Wager was charged with murder. It was now Christmas day.

The Wager's son Benjamin, who was 12 years old on this day, took himself to the dam to examine the foot prints in the clay. Doctor Wrench of Baslow examined the body and found broken bones in Harriet's mouth. His opinion was that this injury was due to a blow from a heavy boot. He also described Harriet as being very fat with a fatty liver 'caused by habits of drinking'. The inspector testified that when Harriet was taken out of the water her head was bald. It was found that she normally wore a wig.

The jury did not accept that she had drowned herself and they gave a verdict of 'guilty with a recommendation to mercy'. The judge donned the black cap and sentenced Wager to be hanged. This was later commuted to life imprisonment; life meant life in those days.

Poison at Rushton Spencer

Poison has always been considered a woman's method of killing people, men tend to use physical violence in its many guises.

In 1818, Jane Grant was set on at a local mill at Litton. Another local girl, Hannah Bocking had already been turned down at the mill because of 'her un-amiable temper and disposition'. This 16 year old servant girl was bent on revenge.

On a Summer's day in 1818 whilst feigning good will Hannah went for a walk with Jane Grant and they arrived at the Gibbet located at a nearby cross roads, which at this time contained the skeleton of Anthony Lingard.

Domestic Strife

Hannah produced a piece of cake which Jane was glad to consume. Shortly afterwards Jane died; poison had been added to the cake.

After being arrested, Hannah was taken to the gaol where she was tried for murder. Knowing what lay ahead for her should she be found guilty she tried to involve her family in the murder, but to no avail. She then admitted that she had bought the poison ten weeks beforehand.

Hannah was found guilty of murder and was hanged in public in front of the County Court using the horse and cart method. She died four days after her trial on 22nd March, 1819.

The local newspaper recorded that, 'At the moment, when she was launched into eternity, an involuntary shuddering pervaded the assembled crowd, and although she excited little sympathy, a general feeling of horror was expressed that one so young should have been so guilty and so insensible'.

Coal Pit murders

This must rank as one of the most brutal multiple murders to have take place in the area of north Derbyshire.

Albert Burrows and Hannah Calladine (Glossop Heritage Centre)

The perpetrator, Albert Edward Burrows was originally from Cheadle Hulme in Cheshire and in 1871 he had an early criminal record for the theft of horses, larceny, assault and cruelty to animals whilst working as a labourer. On the outbreak of World War I in 1914, he managed to gain well paid employment at a munitions factory in Northwich, Cheshire. At the time he had a family comprising a wife and child which he left at home at Back Kershaw Street, Glossop. Whilst in Northwich he became attracted to a younger woman, Hannah Calladine with whom he had a child. On 27th May 1918, they married, Burrows bigamously, having told her that his first wife had died and his child from this marriage was cared for by a house keeper in Glossop.

During his work at Northwich, Burrows was earning good money and he was sending an allowance to his wife in Glossop as well as to his second wife. The end of hostilities also meant the end of George's well paid employment, such that he could not keep up the payments to his two wives. Hanna was getting suspicious about his Glossop connection and she wrote to Burrows's daughter and as a result Burrows was charged with bigamy and was sent to prison for six months at Walton Gaol, Manchester. On leaving prison he went to live with his first wife in Glossop and Hannah took out an affiliation order against Burrows, which he could not pay. She then took out a committal order, as the result of which he was sent to prison in Shrewsbury for twenty-one days.

Burrows had his back to the wall. He could not pay the two women who could both get committal orders, which would mean prison again. Meanwhile, Burrows kept in touch with Hannah and it was arranged that on leaving prison he would live with her. She told her parents that they were going to live in Glossop along with her own son Albert and an illegitimate daughter named Elsie Large. Her parents tried to stop this move without success. On the night of 19 September, 1919 she arrived at Burrows's door and amidst complaints from his first wife she was allowed to stay because the weather was too foul to venture outside. His wife left the following day and Hannah left after three weeks.

His wife sued for maintenance which Burrows could not pay and he already owed on his rent. He had seemingly overcome his problems by the time he attended court on 12th January, 1920. He advised the court that Hannah and the children had left his house. Burrows's first wife returned four days later after Burrows had told her that Hannah had found well paid employment at Seymour Meads, Stretford Road, Manchester adding that the children were being cared for at a creche. This happened to be the last time they were ever seen alive again.

Domestic Strife

At six o'clock on the same morning a witness saw Burrows walking down Hollincross Lane, Glossop with Elsie Large and two hours later he was seen walking back on his own. With Hannah supposedly working in Manchester, Burrows disposed of her few possessions and sold her wedding ring. The situation seems to have returned to normal but on the 9th March the local newspaper reported that Tommy Wood of 96, Backshaw Street, opposite to Burrows's house, had wandered off in the morning of the previous Sunday. He customarily went to his grandmother's home for lunch but did not arrive.

The police and many neighbours undertook a search of the area. Someone said that he had seen Tommy in the company of two boys down Slatelands Road. A search was made in the area, particularly the Turnlee Brook which had swollen by heavy rain, the assumption being that Tommy might have been drowned and swept away. Over the next few days the search continued with the help of dogs.

Burrows assisted the police and made a statement to Inspector Chadwick to the effect that a purse had been found in a chicken pen and a boot print on the bank of the brook which matched Burrows's boot

The search for bodies at Glossop (Glossop Heritage Centre)

print. Burrows tried all manner of excuses for these finds hoping that this might steer the police away from him. Witnesses came forward because of the publicity. A woman stated that she had seen a man with a boy clambering over the shale tips near Coal Pit Close. On the same day a farm worker saw Burrows at Bridgfields with a little boy in hand. Burrows made a statement to explain his movements stating that he had taken the boy for a walk to the fields near Simmondley and climbed the Moss near Hargate Hill, leaving the boy in a hollow to allow Burrows to catch a rabbit. When he returned the boy was not where he had left him and he returned home.

Based on this the police decided to plumb a deserted mine shaft off the Simmondley to Charlesworth road. The shaft was surrounded by an inadequate and damaged fence. A grappling iron was used but the rope broke and the iron was lost. This shaft was about 32 metres deep with water standing in the bottom. It was noted by the Inspector that Burrows was helping with the search. He kept indicating to the police to search at different places away from the shaft. The Inspector then noted that there was another shaft across the road from the first one. This shaft top was protected by a stone wall, part of which had been pulled down recently. The police, with new ropes, assembled at this second shaft (an air shaft for Dinting Pit), over which they laid planks, and by using a grappling iron they soon pulled out the body of a small boy. It was Tommy Wood. The inspector had seen Burrows hiding on the moor and had arranged for him to be watched. His arrest was then ordered and the police had to pursue him with ample help from the public. He was eventually captured in a field known as Garside's Intake in Herod Clough. He was dragged from underneath a holly bush in an exhausted state. The mob had tried to hang him with a red scarf and the police had to rescue him, sending him to Glossop Police Station on the back of a lorry from the Sanitary Department. The streets were lined with people, which was normally only seen when royalty came by. The abuse was endless and loud. Burrows defied the crowds by shaking his handcuffed fists at them and exclaiming 'I shan't tremble on the scaffold like Charlie Peace'.

The inspector questioned Burrows at some length and asked of the whereabouts of Hannah Calladine and her two children. The police were then sent down the shaft where Tommy had been found. As there was water at the bottom they first had to bail it out using a bucket. In spite of this crude method they made progress, however the heavy rain which followed flooded the shaft again. A steam pump was then used which lowered the water rapidly. Human remains were revealed, which when raised to the daylight were declared to be those of a woman. Further bones were found which were discovered to be of two children: a four year old girl and an infant. The skeleton was easily proved to be that of Hannah Calladine by the presence of an abnormal eye tooth and from clothing, confirmed as belonging to Hannah by her sister Elizabeth and a child's clogs were recognised by a clog maker of Nantwich who had made them.

Burrows was sent for trial at the County Assizes in Derby the charge being that he had murdered Hannah Calladine aged thirty-two and her son Albert Edward Burrows aged fifteen months. Mr Justice Shearman presided. As Inspector Chadwick's investigations were so thorough, the trial did not take long and the jury took only fifteen minutes to find Burrows guilty of the charge of murder. The judge donned the black cap and pronounced the death penalty by hanging. The murders of Thomas Wood and Elsie Large were overlooked as Burrows had already been found guilty of other murders and was ordained to hang. At 8 o'clock in the morning of 8th August, 1923, Burrows was hanged at Bagthorpe Gaol, Nottingham.

The remains of Hannah and her children were buried in Glossop Cemetery with a wooden cross to mark the spot. The writer could find no trace of the pits from where the bodies were recovered.

Buried alive

We all dread the thought of being buried alive, much less a possibility today with cremation being popular and the use of sophisticated forensic science.

Thomas Meakyn of Rushton Spencer between Leek and Macclesfield was given the job of caring for horses for a chemist at Stone in Staffordshire, at a time when the horse was the only motive power for farmers and goods. The chemist's daughter made advances to Thomas which he rejected. His employer was aware of this friendship and noted that the affection was one sided.

Thomas was taken ill and quickly died. He was buried in 1781 in Saint Michael's Churchyard at Stone. Soon afterwards people questioned why a healthy young man should die, questioning his employer's action given that he had legal access to poisons. Nothing could be found to support the accusation against the chemist but someone did notice that Thomas's pony had been pawing at his grave for three nights and two days as if digging towards his deceased master.

A year after the interment it was decided that the grave should be opened. They raised the coffin to the surface and the first thing noticed was that Thomas was face down, he had been buried with his face up as is the custom. The report stated that Thomas was buried having been given a drug that made him appear to be dead. It was agreed that the murderer was the chemist but they could not find enough evidence to prosecute him.

His remains were taken to Rushton Spencer where he was buried a second time in the churchyard of Saint Lawrence the Martyr where there is now a murder stone in his memory facing in the opposite direction to the other headstones and inscribed 'As a man falters before wicked men, so fell I'.

Passion

George Fox
George Fox the founder of The Society of Friends' also known as the Quaker movement was arrested in Derby in the month of October, 1650. His offence was blasphemy and he was twenty six years of age.

He was judged by two magistrates; Gervase Bennett and Colonel Nathaniel Barton. It would appear that Bennett had cross examined Fox for eight hours, the Colonel being no more than an onlooker. Furthermore, Bennett had a gift with the words of the English language. The naming of the members of the society as Quakers was to occur during the arraignment of Fox on 30 October, 1650. Fox himself wrote that he had spoken to the magistrates bidding them to 'Tremble like the word of the Lord,' to which Bennett responded 'Quakers', and the name stuck. It was rumoured that Bennett's full response was 'Quaking like frogs in the hands of God'.

With only six months left of his gaol sentence, the recruiting sergeant visited the prison looking for volunteers to join their battle against King Charles II at Worcester in September, 1651, their reward was their liberty afterwards. The prisoners agreed asking that Fox be their Captain. This he refused to do, stating, 'I told them I lived in the virtue of that life and power which took away the occasion of all wars'. He was released in the Winter of the same year.

Bennett died in 1660 at the age of forty nine, having been the Mayor of Derby, its Member of Parliament and surviving three wives. Fox died in 1691 at the age of sixty-seven.

Murder at the Grange
George Victor Townley was a man without hope and his trial caused a national sensation. He was born in 1838, the son of a Manchester merchant and he showed artistic promise at an early age. Before he was five years of age he could play the piano well and spoke fluent French and Latin. Why should he, with his background and talents end up in prison?

He proved to be a disappointment to his father who had apprenticed him to another firm and gave him a job at his own business as a clerk. George was highly strung with a pessimistic outlook on life. It was shown that he had no aptitude for office work and his mother and sister took care of him. In 1859 the family was visited by the Goodwin family

George Victor Townley and Elizabeth 'Bessy' Goodwin (Glossop Heritage Centre)

including their daughter Bessie. George was attracted to her and to a lesser extent she to him. George was twenty-one years of age and Bessie nineteen. The relationship grew and they became engaged to marry.

Then in 1861, two years after they met, Bessie broke off the engagement. They continued to correspond however and, after a meeting in 1862, they became engaged again. Bessie had already gone to live with her grandfather, Captain Goodwin, at Wigwell Grange – it was named Wigwell Hall at this time – at Wirksworth Moor in the Parish of Alderwasley. Bessie's parents visited the Grange in September, 1862 and George's sister in 1863. The Townleys were anticipating a marriage between the two families when a letter arrived from Bessie in August, 1863 breaking the engagement yet again. This decision was made at her mother's suggestion because of George's instability and as Bessie was seeing a young clergyman who had visited Wigwell Grange. George sank into a deep melancholia, weeping and refusing food and drink. His parents were so alarmed that they employed a man to sit with him overnight. He did not enjoy George's company as he spent the night weeping. Next day George wrote to Bessie asking that they should meet once more before they parted forever. Bessie was not enamoured with this idea and she wrote to George telling him to stay away.

For reasons unknown they continued their correspondence and a meeting was arranged. He immediately caught a train from Manchester to Derby where he stayed at the Midland Hotel next to the station. He took a train to Whatstandwell from Derby. On arrival George left his bag in the care of the landlady of the Bull Inn. He then walked the five miles to Wirksworth, passing the Grange on his way. He then called at the Grammar School to speak with the head teacher, Reverend Herbert Harris to ask about his rival. Harris responded by telling George that any such information could not be disclosed. George then decided to confront Bessie. This he did at about six o'clock in the evening. Bessie was called for and the couple set out on a walk. Thirty minutes later they were sitting on a garden seat in the adjoining spinney. A housemaid turned up bearing a message for Bessie. The hapless couple decided to go for a longer walk leaving the grounds of the grange turning onto a lane where George made one desperate plea for a reconciliation. Bessie refused and after an argument he cut her throat with a pocket knife.

Reuben Conway, a labourer who happened to be close by helped George to carry Bessie to the grange. George kissed her but she was bleeding to death and died before they reached the grange. Captain Goodwin, now in his nineties, was overwhelmed by the sight which met him and he suggested that they have a cup of tea!

The police were sent for and they arrested George and placed him in the lock-up at Wirksworth. On 24 August, 1863 the coroner's inquest returned a verdict of murder and George was taken to the County Gaol in Derby, pending a trial at the assizes. The trial was held on 11 December, 1863 presided over by Baron Martin, the crown being represented by Messrs Boden and Bristowe. George's defence was conducted by Messrs. Macauley, Fitzjames Stephen and Sergeant O'Brien. The defence was that George was insane at the time of the stabbing. Macauley called numerous witnesses to support this and relatives gave evidence that mental instability was present in his antecedents. Forbes Winslow, an eminent psychiatric doctor told the court that George believed that he had committed no sin and all he was interested in was property stolen from him. The surgeon at the County Gaol stated that George was unaware of what he had done. He stated 'I consider him to be of unsound mind'.

The jury found George guilty and the sentence of death was passed on him. The Judge, along with many in the court, was sobbing throughout the sentencing. A campaign was started with a view of getting the sentence commuted. Petitions were raised comprising: Manchester 16,000 signatures, 300 from the area round Wigwell and over 300 from Derby. Nine of the jurors wrote to the Home Secretary.

Baron Martin wrote to Sir George Grey, Home Secretary, stating George's defence had been insanity and suggesting further investigations. Three Lunacy Commissioners were appointed to examine George. His defence council then found a rare Act stating that medical men and magistrates are allowed to examine prisoners where mental illness was cited as a cause of behaviour. Five men were appointed to examine George including the Mayor, Thomas Roe and Doctor Harwood, surgeon to the Poor Law Union. They all declared that George was insane. The Lunacy Commissioners had also reported to Grey that whilst George was capable of knowing what he had done was wrong, he was not of sound mind.

Grey sent George to Bethlem or Bedlem Hospital (this institution in London was the only one for criminally insane people). The real name was Bethlehem Hospital. The site was where Liverpool Street Station now stands. By George's time it had been relocated to where the Imperial War Museum now stands. His final years were spent at Pentonville Prison. The populace would visit the Bedlam Hospital to be entertained by the demonic behaviour of its inmates. Broadmoor Hospital for the Criminally Insane came later.

This caused a national furore. This trial and its outcome was viewed by the working classes as a good example of class discrimination and not without reason. At the same time as the events surrounding George's reprieve a Samuel Wright had murdered his wife during a dispute. Between arrest and hanging was just a week. The spectators at his hanging booed and jeered the hangman with shouts of 'Where's Townley'. A leaflet was distributed which stated 'Shall Wright be hung? If so then there is one law for the rich and another for the poor'.

Sadly, after George had been sent to Pentonville Prison he committed suicide by jumping over the stair case. Bessie has a memorial stone in the church of Saint Mary the Virgin, Wirksworth which tells us that she died on 21st August, 1863 at the age of twenty-two years. It also tells us that she was the daughter of Henry and Agnes Goodwin. She is buried in the Goodwin Family Vault.

Passion

The Padley Martyrs
In the reign of Queen Elizabeth I, to practice the religion of Roman Catholicism was punishable by death. Three priests: Nicholas Garlick, a school master at Tideswell, Richard Sympson and Robert Ludlum, from near Sheffield, were all accused of 'trying to seduce Her Majesty's people'. The price they had to pay was being sentenced to hanging, drawing and quartering.

The then Earl of Shrewsbury, as the Lord Lieutenant of the County, had entered the Padley Estate, near Hathersage in pursuit of the Fitzherbert family to arrest them for following the church of Rome. Instead they arrested Nicholas Garlick and Robert Ludlum who were hiding in a chimney at Padley Hall. It was said that the priests had held services at what is now known as Padley Chapel, close to the hall. At this time this chapel was a gate house where the Fitzherberts worshipped, using it as an improvised church. They were transported to the gaol at Derby where they met another priest Richard Sympson, a convert to the faith who was in the process of denouncing his conversion to save his neck. The three

Padley Chapel

men decided that they would keep the faith regardless of the punishment they might have to face.

They were all found guilty of High Treason and on 24th July, 1588 they met the cruel fate of being hung, drawn and quartered on St Mary's Bridge, Derby. This started by dragging them on hurdles with the three men upside down and backwards behind horses to the execution site. One witness stated that Nicholas Garlic was conscious during the drawing part of his sentence. Their heads were placed on pikes at Saint Mary's Bridge as a warning to others. The body parts were displayed around Derby for the same reason. Tradition has it that Garlick's head was buried during the night in Tideswell graveyard. Before he died Garlick preached the Catholic faith to the onlookers.

For harbouring the priests, John Fizherbert, who resided at and owned Padley Hall, was sentenced to hang but died of jail fever in the Fleet Prison, London.

Padley Hall was demolished in 1650 and the gate house became a farmer's barn. It was acquired by Monsignor Ashton Shuttleworth in 1931 and was bought by Monsignor Charles Payne on behalf of the Nottingham Catholic Diocese in 1933. It was restored and consecrated a year later. It is now shared between the dioceses of Hallam (Sheffield) and Nottingham. A childrens' pilgrimage is held annually on the Thursday prior to 17th July and a Diocesan pilgrimage is held on the Sunday nearest to 12 July.

The Chapel is open to visitors from late April to late September, on Wednesdays and Sundays, between 2.00 and 4.00 pm.

A duel at Winster

The Brittlebank family were well known in Winster during the nineteenth century as lead merchants and lawyers, living at Oddo House and later at Winster Hall. In 1821 there were three Brittlebanks: William Senior and Junior and Mary. The local medical practitioner, Doctor William Cuddie, aged thirty-one years, had taken a fancy to Mary, a sentiment returned by her. The doctor was known for his humanity; he often dispensed drugs to the poor free of charge and helped desperate people with cash hand outs.

Mary's brother had seen the couple together and had tried to keep them apart. The upshot of this was a heated argument between the two men. Later the doctor was in receipt of a note from William which read: 'Sir, I expect satisfaction for the insult you dared to offer me at a time when you knew that my situation with a helpless woman prevented my chastising you. Name your time and place, the bearer will wait for an answer.

Sir, Yours, & c.
William Brittlebank, Jun.
I shall be attended by a friend with pistols, and if you don't meet I shall post you as a coward.'

Cuddie chose to ignore this and a reply was not sent. The following afternoon, the Brittlebank brothers appeared in his garden with two loaded pistols, or were they? Cuddie accepted the challenge albeit with hesitation and was handed one of the pistols. Brittlebank walked fifteen yards away, turned and fired. There were two shots heard and Cuddie was wounded but not so Brittlebank. Cuddie died the following day. Williams Senior and Junior along with an accomplice, Edmund Spencer, were charged with murder, All were found not guilty due to a technicality. William Junior had already run away and a price of £100 was placed on his head. It is said that he emigrated to Australia and never returned. There were supposed sightings at Liverpool and Brighton without result. It was also rumoured that Cuddie's pistol had not been loaded. A letter was found in the pocket of Cuddie's coat written by Mary which partly read: 'My eternal peace depends on you not seeing any of our family they are quite bent on shooting. For mercy's sake, keep out of their way'. If only the good doctor had taken heed of this.

We will come across a Brittlebank in 'The Magpie Murders'.

Murder on a boat

John Cotton, a Bargee, beat his wife to death in his boat at Bugsworth Canal Basin near Stockport. The woman was 36 years of age and the cause of the crime was due to Cotton's jealousy. He had used a poker, hitting her on the head and fractured the base of her skull.

He was tried at the Derby Assizes where his defence was that he had been provoked. This did not wash and he was sentenced to death by hanging. After being sentenced Cotton had displayed contrition and had taken great interest in all the chaplain had to say. The day prior to the sentence being carried out, Cotton paid constant attention to the chaplain and after a bad night he was administered to by the chaplain again. At 8.00 am, Cotton was taken to the gallows to be met by the executioner who pinioned his arms. His ankles were secured when he was facing the gallows. The executioners were Billington and his son, the latter getting ready to take over from his father when he retired. Cotton was composed throughout the process. The chaplain recited the words, 'Remember not the offences of thy servants' after which the drop was activated and

Cotton was dead. On examination it was found that death had been instantaneous.

A crowd had gathered outside the prison to witness the hoisting of the black flag. There was no sympathy for the prisoner, who it was revealed had murdered two previous wives. Cotton was 66 years of age at the time, 30 years older than his late wife.

The tragedy of Joan Waste

Joan Waste lived in Derby. She was blind but she was capable of helping her father, a rope maker, and she was a skilful knitter before she was 12 years of age. She was also very religious and an ardent follower of Protestantism and was able to navigate the streets to access the churches in Derby. She also visited an old man regularly who languished in a Debtor's Cell in Derby Prison. He read to Mary and taught her many things to satisfy her curiosity. She also employed a John Pemerton in her quest for knowledge.

Queen Mary acceded to the throne of England in 1553 when Joan was 22 years of age. She clung to her beliefs and refused to accept the Roman Catholic faith. She was tried and sentenced to death by burning as a heretic. After spending five weeks in prison she was taken to All Saints' Church (now Derby Cathedral) where a Doctor Draycott preached a sermon in which he denounced Joan, saying that not only was she physically blind but spiritually blind also. She was handed over to the Bailiffs and on the first day of August 1556 she was sentenced to be burnt at the stake. She was led to the place of execution, the Windmill Pit, her sisters supporting her with prayers and she held her brother's hand as she was led from the church. She died at the stake, a hideous death, begging for mercy from Christ.

When Queen Mary died, and her half sister Elizabeth ascended the throne, the tables turned and Protestantism was reintroduced. Elizabeth was as zealous in persecuting Catholic heretics as Mary had been in persecuting Protestants.

It is said that the site where Joan died is haunted by her. One assumes that the site of the execution is somewhere near to Windmill Hill Lane, Derby.

A poisoning

The use of poison to kill someone was generally accepted as the method preferred by women. This was certainly the case here.

John Hewit of Derby was a butcher and a married man. He was

beguiled by a servant to the widowed landlady of the Crown Public House at Nun's Green, Derby. When confessing, Hewit told how he had carnal knowledge of the landlady and the servant.

The landlady was also beguiled by John Hewit and was intent on marrying him. To this end she prepared a lethal meal of a poisoned pancake which she fed to Mrs Hewit. The poor woman complained of stomach pains and vomited up the meal which a pig promptly devoured. The pig died followed by the death of Mrs Hewit after three hours of agony. Whilst Mrs Hewit suffered the agony of poisoning, the landlady was contentedly undertaking the ironing of some clothes in the parlour. The landlady avoided prosecution but not so Mr Hewit and Rosamond Oderenshaw the servant. They were proved to have been accessories to the act. Before she died on the scaffold, Rosamund confessed that a few weeks prior she had been persuaded by the landlady to administer poison to Mrs Hewit's broth. There was insufficient poison to cause a fatality. She also admitted to having borne Hewit's child which she killed and buried. She gave a precise location of the burial place and after excavating it the bones of a seven months old child were uncovered.

They provided each other with a shroud in which they walked to the gallows. They were penitent and confessed their guilt before being hanged on 20th March, 1732.

A horrible murder at Agard Street

Agard Street is an old thoroughfare in Derby, linking Bridge Street and Ford Street.

This is a story of a flirt and the jealousy she aroused. Eliza Barrow was friendly with a Richard Thorley, a boxer and a striker in a factory. But Eliza had a penchant for flirting with the soldiers billeted in Agard Street. Richard would retaliate by punching and generally abusing Eliza.

In January Thorley beat her seriously, such that she banned him from her presence, telling him that their friendship was over.

On 13th February, 1862, he harassed her by beating a drum outside her window, calling, 'Come on, let's have a look at the soldier you're in bed with tonight'. Eliza shut her window forcefully. Thorley repaired to his lodging to get his razor. On returning to Eliza's home he broke in and cut her throat. She bled profusely much of which was deposited on Thorley's coat. He resorted to a tavern and needing an excuse he told the barman that he had been in a fight with a gang of Irishmen.

He was apprehended and charged with wilful murder and appeared in the dock on Monday, 24th March, 1862 before Mr Justice Williams. This

THE MURDERER.

RICHARD THORLEY,
Executed at Derby, April 11th, 1862.

HIS VICTIM.

ELIZA MORROW,
Murdered at Derby, February 13th, 1862.

Richard Thorley and Elizabeth Morrow

trial created a huge amount of interest with the citizens of Derby and the authorities decided that proposed attendees should procure tickets to gain admission. Between six and seven o'clock, there was a large crowd waiting outside the court, mostly women. When the doors were eventually opened the spaces inside the court were soon filled. A large crowd remained outside the court all day regardless of the cold and wet weather.

Thorley took his place in the dock and was told to enter a plea to which he replied 'Not Guilty'. As there had been much gossip and rumour surrounding this case the judge advised the jury to stick to the evidence and ignore everything else. Witnesses were called and examined and it became clear that Thorley was guilty, a verdict arrived at by the jury whose deliberations only lasted a few minutes. Thorley was calm throughout the trial and up to his hanging.

Richard Thorley was hanged on 11th April, 1862 outside the prison and in public, the last such public hanging outside this prison on Vernon Street, Derby; ironically near to the scene of his murdering Eliza Barrow.

He was buried in the precincts of the prison as was the fashion in those days.

Ronald Smedley

Smedley is a common name locally in and around Matlock including John Smedley, the founder of Hydropathy who had a large 'Hospital' on Matlock Bank. Research might prove a connection between them. Ronald lived at Bolehill, a community overlooking Wirksworth and backing onto Cromford Moor and Forest. Ronald was employed as a labourer at a firebrick maker located on the summit of Carsington Pastures, near Brassington. These refractory bricks were destined for the steel industry at Sheffield where they were used for lining retorts.

Jessie Ball had been 'walking out' with Ronald from Spring, 1936 onwards. Ronald would visit her at the home she shared with her parents, Quarry Cottage near to the Slack, a steep highway between Kelstedge and Matlock Forest, the main road between Chesterfield and Matlock. Ronald was 25 years old at the time and Jessie two years younger. He visited her on every Wednesday, Friday and Sunday, bringing small gifts for her each time. On Friday, 20th August, 1937, Jessie was left alone to await Ronald's arrival whilst her parents visited elsewhere, comforted with the thought that Jessie would soon be cared for by Ronald. They noticed that the bus from Matlock had arrived at the top of the Slack knowing that Ronald would be on it. Jessie's cousin Florence Bowen arrived from her parents home, Amber Lane Cottage, Kelstedge near to the bottom of the Slack where the River Amber flowed, hence the name of the cottage. Florence was admitted to the Quarry Cottage to be met by Jesse and Ronald who was sitting on a sofa. All seemed convivial as they ate the chocolates brought by Ronald. Jessie's parents, James and Marion Ball arrived home near to midnight. There was something amiss at the cottage. The garden gate which was always kept shut was swinging open and was damaged. The cottage was in darkness and Marion shouted for Jessie without a reply. After lighting a lamp, she noticed that the table had been tipped over in the front room and the items which had been left on the table were scattered on the floor including Ronald's chocolates. A search of the entire cottage produced nothing, however, James ventured into the rear garden and found his daughter's body. She had been badly bruised about the head and she was dead.

The Doctor soon arrived to find that Jessie also had a nasty wound to her forehead which had bled profusely. There was blood scattered on the garden. A man's tie was round her neck coupled with foaming mucus about her mouth. The Doctor's first reaction was that she had been strangled to death. The matter had now spread into the following day. Smedley was the prime suspect and the police soon arrived at his door on Bolehill. His bed had not been used and the occupants did not know where he might be.

A search was instituted using blood hounds borrowed from a Mr C.A. Furness of Brampton Hall near Chesterfield with a detailed description sent to the local press. All to no avail. Ponds were dragged and moorland searched in the event that Smedley might have taken his own life. The Police issued another plea for help in finding him.

The 25th August was a sad day for many people when Jessie was buried in the churchyard at the Parish Church at Ashover with the Curate officiating. On the same day there was a sighting of Smedley running away from Riber Hillside Farm. Both serious and dubious sightings were now flooding in. A woman reported a man jumping from a tree in Willersley Castle woods, Cromford, who then ran away. A man was approached in Derby by a scruffy man asking where he could get a shave. The Police arrived at the barber's chair to find that this was the wrong man. 500 posters were distributed and more 'sightings' were reported from places as far away as Wales.

The breakthrough came on 1st September when a labourer, Thomas Hopkinson of Moor Edge Farm, Tansley, a village near Matlock had witnessed a man following him along a lane on Sunday, 29th August; he fitted the description of Smedley. On the 30th August Hopkinson found twenty empty corn sacks made into a crude bed in a barn at the bottom of this lane. The next day a Mr Swift reported that there was a sleeping man in a haystack at his farm at Cromford. The Police arrived and arrested Smedley, he had been on the run for twelve days. He was hand cuffed and taken to Matlock Police Station.

The Pathologist's Report revealed that Jessie was pregnant. Her mother told the court that Smedley and her daughter had become engaged to be married. Smedley had made a written statement to the effect that he believed that Florence was walking out with another man, Harry Ludlum of Matlock. A friend of Smedley's from childhood told the court that when cycling to work one morning his friend said that he was in trouble and would have to marry Jessie. Smedley when in the dock told the jury that Jessie had pointed to her stomach and said that her pregnancy was due to either Smedley or Ludlum.

The jury returned a verdict of guilty but with a recommendation for mercy. Mr Justice McNaughton had no choice but to pronounce the penalty of death by hanging. Smedley was transferred to Leicester Prison to await his death. A petition for mercy was signed by 5,000 people and Smedley's solicitor, Mr Mather, delivered the petition by hand to the Home Office. On 29th November, 1937 the King commuted Smedley's punishment to life imprisonment.

Footnote: The author has always been fascinated by this murder as it all took place in the area where he has lived for thirty years. Ronald Smedley along with many other prisoners in his Majesty's prisons, was invited to join the Army for special duties. Their likelihood of survival was small but many took their chances, including Smedley. The pay off for survivors was a possible, but not certain, release from custody. Smedley joined the army and lived to return to a post war Britain with a pardon. He continued to live at Bolehill, married and had a son John. One of the writer's homes was near to Bolehill where he would see Ronald walking along the lane in a strict outfit of overcoat, hat and clean shoes for his daily constitutional. His son John did labouring work locally and became a physically powerful man just like his father. The author often meets John in Wirksworth and spends a little time talking to him about his father. The Mathers are still solicitors in Chesterfield.

Daylight Robbery

They hang 'em in bunches in Heage

Heage, short for its original name High Edge, sits on a plateau above the river Derwent and is east of Belper.

Two elderly spinsters, Sarah and Martha Goddard, lived at Stanley Hall, an isolated house where they kept themselves to themselves and lived the lives of hermits. They were easy prey for thieves. William Scattergood, a nearby farmer, was roused from his bed by an urgent knocking on his door. To his surprise Sarah Goddard from the hall stood outside in a distressed condition, she was covered in blood from a gash on her head and she also had a broken finger. Scattergood made his way to the hall and on arrival ran upstairs to see if the other sister, Martha, was safe. He looked on a dreadful sight. She was spread on her bed with wounds to her scalp and her skull had been fractured. There was evidence of blows to her head from a blunt instrument. A Doctor Bowden was called who examined Martha but there was little he could do and she soon expired in his presence a little later.

A hunt for the perpetrators led the police to John Hulme, Samuel Bonsall and William Bland who lived close to each other in Heage. Hulme's neighbour was a needle maker named Joseph Simpson, who questioned Hulme advising him that he was a suspect for the murder. Hulme denied any involvement in the matter. He decided to question Richard Dronfield, Hulme's apprentice. He said that he had seen Dronfield on his chimney sweeping round in Idridgehay, a nearby village. He had seen Hulme and Bonsall on the morning of the murder carrying a lady's clothes. Bland joined them and they decided to hide the clothes until later when it was quieter. Simpson then took Dronfield to a sough – a lead mining draining tunnel, possibly the Fritchley one – near Ambergate, where several articles were recovered. Simpson visited John Hawkins, the Parish Constable and they searched the homes of Bonsall and Bland finding even more clothes. They were taken into custody on 4th October, 1842. Hulme made a run for it to his mother's house in Leek, Staffordshire and then on to Marston Wood, using it as a hide out. A few days later, Hulme enquired of his mother if he was in danger, she promptly went to see the local constable and Hulme was arrested.

The trial was on 26th March, 1843 before Mr Baron Gurney. The prosecution was undertaken by Sergeant Clark and Messrs. Whitehurst and Fowler. Hulme alone employed defence council, a Mr Miller. Their guilt was a foregone conclusion as they all had clothing taken from Stanley Hall. As individuals they each admitted being present at the Hall. Hulme and Bland signed depositions blaming Bonsall for delivering the fatal blows with a crowbar. Bonsall of course rejected this claim saying that Bland did the deed. They now realised that they would be found guilty and to avoid hanging they tried to blame each other.

Mr Hutchinson, the Clerk to the Magistrates, told the court that a promise of pardon had been made to any accomplice, except the one who actually committed the murder.

Evidence was given by several people; A farmer, Joseph Roe had met two men on the Stanley to Heage road at 2.30 in the morning when he met the defendants. Roe thought they might have been poaching and he asked the men to show him what was inside their bags. They then offered violence and Roe went away in fear of his life.

John Brown and William Salt shared a cell (and a bed!) with Bonsall. They testified that Bonsall had admitted his guilt.

These witnesses sealed Bonsall's fate along with his accomplices. Council for Bonsall tried to persuade the jury that the witnesses statements were unreliable. This did not wash with either the jury or the Judge. The jury took only ten minutes to find the prisoners guilty.

The Judge, Baron Gurney, made the following statement: 'I consider the guilt of all three of you as one, and the same. The sentence of this court is that you be taken to the place from whence you came, and from thence to a place of execution, and that you be severally hanged until you are dead and your bodies buried within the precincts of the gaol. And may God have mercy on your souls'. Bonsall then cried out to the court 'There is no God'.

This formula was used by most judges when sentencing the guilty to be hung.

31st March was the date chosen for the public hanging. The men confessed on the scaffold that this was not the first time they had flouted the law. Bonsall and Hulme had previously robbed a man named Fletcher of Pentrich whilst on the Queen's highway and had broken into his mill to plunder it. Bonsall and Brand named Hulme as the ringleader and that he alone carried the blame for their present dilemma. His two brothers were at this time abroad after being transported.

Finally Bonsall admitted that he was the killer, the others had beaten the victim.

A huge crowd gathered before the gallows on 31st March, 1843, the local press giving the number as forty to fifty thousand.

The executioner was Mr Haywood of Appleby-in-Westmorland and he undertook his duties professionally. Bonsall died instantly but before he dropped he was seen to be praying and cried out 'Lord have mercy upon me, Christ have mercy'.

The Trial and Execution
OF
Samuel Bonsell, aged 26, William Bland, 39, and John Hulme, 24.
Who were hanged on the New Drop, Derby, on Friday, March 31, 1843.
FOR THE HORRID AND COLD-BLOODED
Murder of Martha Goddard, aged 72,
AT THE TOWNSHIP OF STANLEY, DERBYSHIRE.

A broadsheet describing the trial and execution of the Heage men in 1843
Nottingham University Library

John Hulme, Samuel Bonsall and William Bland

The crowd dispersed rapidly for many had trains to catch, two being laid on as a special excursions to witness the hangings. The crowd was also swollen by those who were celebrating the Easter Fair in town that day.

Magpie Mine Murders

Magpie Mine, a lead mine, near Sheldon, has had a mixed existence, from times of plenty to times of poor production; many different people and organisations have tried to make money out of it with little success.

The Magpie Mine title ran close to the title of the Red Soil Mine and disputes became common, each side claiming a right to work the veins. In 1833 the inevitable happened, the Red Soil Miners tried to smoke the intruders out by burning straw and tar (from the gasworks) but the wind changed direction and the Red Soil Men were smoked out instead. The Magpie miners then sought revenge by lighting their own fire of straw with sulphur added and it was reported that the shafts smoked like factory chimneys. Early the next morning the Red Soil agent descended into the mine and declared it as being safe for work to recommence. At a depth of 128 metres some of the miners were overcome by fumes. Water was poured down the shaft to encourage the dispersal of the gases and both sides organised a rescue party. They found three Red Soil men to have died by asphyxiation.

Two days later, the police arrived from Derby and arrested six of the twenty four men deemed to have been involved. Seventeen of the Magpie Miners were also arrested. A Barmote Court held at Ashford-in-the-Water declared angrily that it was a case of murder. This court had the right to be coroners for deaths in lead mines. A trial was opened six month's later at the County Court, Derby when all twenty-four men were charged with murder, as the act was premeditated. Twenty-one of them were found not guilty and were discharged. The remaining three were charged with manslaughter but were found not guilty. They were defended by William Brittlebank of Winster (see 'A Duel').

The arguments put forward were that it was legal to light fires below ground at the end of the mineral day, 1 o'clock in the afternoon and the Agent had been negligent for not descending the workings to a greater depth.

As can be imagined the widows of the dead men were angry with the verdict and legend has it that the they cast a curse on the mine and, strangely or co-incidentally, the mine did not prosper well after this.

The Coterol Gang

This gang is often referred to as the Coterel Gang. The more common spelling of Coterol has been used here.

This gang, active in the 14th century, is well documented in spite of it's activities being so long ago. They were especially active in Yorkshire, Nottinghamshire, Leicestershire and Rutland but predominantly in Derbyshire. Their story parallels Robin Hood and his Merry Men. There were numerous such gangs in this century which caused the country to have a 'lack of governance'.

They were known in 1328 and in 1331 they were outlawed for not appearing in court. James was the leader and his gang became known as the Society of James Coterol. They travelled through the forests of the High Peak and Sherwood. It was known that he had twenty men in the High Peak alone. There were four Coterols at large including James the leader (1328 - 1351), Laurence, John and Nicholas who evaded the law.

In 1326, they murdered Roger Bellars, Baron of the Exchequer. In 1332, they sought a ransom for Sir Richard Willoughby, Justice of the King's Bench. The money for this was shared with another gang, the Folvilles who were members of the household of Sir Robert Tuchet of Markeaton, Derby. They went on to murder Sir William Knyveton (Kniveton, near Ashbourne) and John Matkynson of Bradley (a village close to Ashbourne) in 1330.

By this time James was becoming a figure of folk lore as much as an outlaw. There then started a set of mystical happenings on the right side of the law. James was given the commission to arrest a cleric for an illegal activity, alas, we do not know what this was. Nicholas was appointed by Queen Philippa as her Bailiff of the High Peak. He also led an army of archers to Scotland and, in the image of Falstaff, stole the soldiers wages. Laurence was less fortunate, he was killed by Roger de Wennesley (Wensley), Lord of Mappleton (Staffordshire), who then joined the gang!

These men were not the poor men that one might assume. They all held land which the crown made no effort to sequester. Their rents were paid to them whilst they rampaged across the area. Ralph, a brother of the Coterols enjoyed the rents from Taddington, Priestcliffe, Chelmorton, Flagg, Tunstead and Matlock.

They imprisoned people and claimed fines for their release varying from £5 to £40. One such was the ransom paid for Sir Richard Willoughby Junior which was paid to the gang at Markeaton Park, just north of Derby. Such payments were shared amongst the gang members. This ransom was 1300 marks (£867) but only 340 were given to the gang.

Sir Robert Ingram backed the Coterols and employed them for nefarious duties including the household of the Dean and Chapter of Lichfield, Staffordshire.

Their activities were varied and they did service to many who needed a reliable private army to help them. Their area of influence covered mostly the Peak District of Derbyshire with a lesser amount in north Nottinghamshire in Robin Hood territory. All in all they led a charmed life, robbing, helping the monarchy and undertaking onerous duties for the country and others without apparently killing anyone in the process. They were well led, well organised and numerous, a force to reckon with in a lawless land.

Note: Queen Phillippa of Hainault (1311-69) was the consort of King Edward III. She bore twelve children the second of which was to become the Black Prince.

George Woodcock – also known as Omar Shamgar

George is included as he was one of the few in the Victorian era to be sent from Derbyshire to Dartmoor Prison.

On 3rd June, 1856, Omar was found guilty at Derby Assizes of an unrecorded offence and was sent to Dartmoor Prison to serve 10 years of penal servitude. He was free two years later after escaping. He was apprehended at York and was sent back to Dartmoor Prison. The Prior Warden travelled to York to identify him and to advise the authorities that Omar had been admitted on 25th September, 1854 and on 25th August, 1855. George had escaped by crawling down a drain which was reputed to have been a mile long. He stole some clothes and changed into them leaving his prison garb behind him. He was trailed for several days but they lost sight of him.

George would have been called a career criminal today, but he was not unintelligent. He spoke four languages and knew the bible intimately. A summary is given below of his life as it is known; there would not be sufficient space to list this in detail.

- Offences were committed at Aylesbury, Durham, Northampton, Retford (Notts), Bedford and there are more.
- Prison terms apart from Dartmoor were several in France, Preston (broke out twice), York (foiled escape), Aylesbury (1847 – stealing shoes – a month), Durham (1848 – 3 months), Leicester (1849 – stealing boots – one month) , Retford (1850 – housebreaking – 12 months) Wakefield (five times), Northampton (1851 – stole boots – 9 months). He boasted that he had been in every prison in England.
- Violence – When at Derby he beat up a fellow prisoner and attacked a warder with a length of wood. At Northampton he was confined in a 'dark cell' for misconduct, placed in irons and flogged, he

GEORGE WOODCOCK

George Woodcock Legendary Dartmoor (Tim Sandles)

scaled a chimney at Preston and had to be smoked out.
- He formed a gang to burgle a house on the banks of the Yorkshire Ouse near York. He had calculated that the gang could have made £2,000 from this venture, a fortune at that time.
- He was convicted for burglary 18 times, a conservative estimate?
- In 1853 he was committed to Bedford Prison for 18 months for burglary. He was violent, attacked the governor, he wrecked his cell and denied access to everyone. He trapped the governor in his cell and threatened him with a knife. George's comment at the time was, 'I will wash my hands in his blood and then destroy myself'.
- He spent time in a 'Lunatic Asylum' where he improved considerably. It was believed that he had improved such that he was 'of a quiet and pious demeanour'. This was to prove erroneous as he escaped soon afterwards.
- He boasted that he had committed every crime other than murder.
- Aliases as well as Woodcock and Shamgar: Massey, Thompson, Montgomery, Sigismund and Colbeck.
- Described himself: 'Born a rogue, brought up a rogue, mean to continue as a rogue'.

One can only speculate long after these events surrounding George that he must have been mentally unstable and with modern drug therapy he might have been cured of his violence.

The confessions of Percival Cooke and James Tomlinson

These two impecunious men would be all but forgotten had it not been that an anonymous person wrote and had published a six page leaflet explaining the background of this story and his distaste at the use of the gallows for such robberies.

Percival Cooke was 26 years old at the time of this tale and he lived at Dale Abbey, near to Ilkeston. He had been apprenticed to a Frame-work Knitter at Nottingham who along with his friends asked for clemency for what was to happen later. Cooke was religious, he had a Methodist upbringing and was a deserter from the Army. Little was known of Tomlinson except that he was born in a village near to Belton in Leicestershire, he too was a Frame-work Knitter and, like Cooke, was a deserter from the Army. These crimes were committed during the last year of the Napoleonic Wars, the famous march to Moscow by Napoleon's Grand Army was to occur before the year was out and the battle of Waterloo occurred three years later in 1815. Routinely at this time deserters were hanged.

There were two indictments:
- they entered the house of a Mr S. How from whom they stole £35 cash, gold guineas, notes and sundry articles.
- they entered the house of a John Bramall of Locko Grange, near Spondon and took nothing after being challenged by the son of the house and one of the servants.

There were others involved in the affair:
- Thomas Draper, who turned King's Evidence
- James Jeram alias Ockbrook Will (Ockbrook is close to Locko)
- A man named Howit Scott also known as Thomas Dundey
- John England of Little Hallam, Ilkeston who was found guilty along with Cooke and Tomlinson.

Cooke and Tomlinson were sentenced to be hung despite pleas for mercy from them both. It was a public hanging and the two prisoners turned their heads to the prison wall so that the public could not witness their last moments on earth.

Cooke left a widow and two young children. Had the Army managed to arrest them before the robbery, they would have been hung as deserters in any event.

The Theft of £400

William Flint, a farmer at Biggin-by-Hartington found himself in arrears with his rent, payable to the Chatsworth Estate. John Dale made a distraining order on Flint on 29th September, 1824 for unpaid rent. Flint had struggled for many years and this situation continued up until 1837 when a Francis Roe was given the task of finding Flint, there being a rumour that he had come into a large sum of money. Roe sent a letter to Peter Pichot, Constable of Hartington whose Headborough (a Petty Constable) was William Flint's brother Mathew. This letter reads as follows:

'I have yours of the first instant and agreeable to your wish made enquiries respecting William Flint. I perceive that he has come in possession of £400. I find this Flint you wish to be informed about has been residing in the Town (London) as a Carter. Since coming into the money he has gone into Wales to purchase Horses. They say he is married again but I could no longer say his place of residence. His brother informed me that this money will soon be gone. I feel that he will not be worthy of powder and shot and from what I hear he is a bad lot.'

It would appear that William was working for Thomas and Matthew Pickford, Carriers of King's Sterndale who were later to create the well known company of carriers known as 'Pickfords'. William worked for the company as a carrier visiting Wales to attend the fairs to buy horses. People being happy to pull a man down could have created all manner of reasons why Flint carried so much money. A more plausible reason could be that he needed the money with which to buy horses for his employer. However, £400 at that time was a fortune and would have bought a large number of horses.

As the oft used saying goes, 'The Jury is still out on this one'.

Charlie Peace

Peace was a well known criminal famous for his exploits, who enjoyed a certain misguided popularity in Victorian England.

He was born in Sheffield on 14th May, 1832 and was named Charles Frederick Peace. His father John Peace was born at Burton-on-Trent, Staffordshire and was a collier. An accident caused him to lose a leg and he joined Bostock and Wombwell's Circus as an animal trainer where he acquired a reputation for this newly acquired skill. John then married, at Rotherham to the daughter of a ship's surgeon. Their first son had acquired his father's skills with wild animals but had died. By the time Charles was born, the youngest of four children, his father was a shoe maker in Sheffield. Charles was sent to two schools where he learned nothing but excelled himself at making paper models, taming cats, constructing a peep show and throwing a ball of lead shot which he then caught in a leather socket fixed to his forehead. He was of small stature, but supple and strong. Charles was apprenticed to the Rolling Mill works but was badly injured when a glowing piece of red hot steel cut through his right leg below the knee, causing him to be hospitalised for 18 months in the Sheffield Infirmary, after which he was left crippled for life. His father died at about this time.

Being unemployable he used his skill at playing the violin at concerts and by hawking bric-a-brac and musical instruments. However this did not pay too well so he took to pretty crime by picking pockets. At the age of 19, he was convicted for stealing a gentleman's gold watch. His next exploit, and we have a date for this, 26th October, 1851, he broke into a lady's house where he stole some goods. He was arrested for being in possession of some of these goods. He was let off lightly and spent a month in prison, his first sentence of many. On release he took up music, teaching himself to play a violin on one string and he became known locally as the 'modern Paganini'. He took up crime again commencing with a round of robbing and other minor crimes and he grew accustomed to spending much of his life in prisons. He still used a violin case in which to carry the tools of his new trade. He became known as the 'portico thief', because his access to a house was by climbing onto its portico. In Sheffield many houses were burgled this way.

He married a widow, Hannah Ward, in 1859 who brought her baby son with her, an event swiftly followed by his residing in Wakefield Prison. On his release six years later he rejoined Hannah. He appeared to be a reformed person. He learned picture framing and he opened a shop at Sheffield. Sadly, he contracted rheumatic fever, a killer at that time. His business failed from lack of attention.

Charlie (as he was now commonly known) started stealing again and he was out to prove that he would be the greatest cat burglar ever. He developed a routine for casing the targeted properties well in advance of his visits. He dressed smartly and carried his tools in a violin case. He wore women's boots during the burglary. He deadened the sound and obscured his foot prints by wearing woollen socks over the boots. He became a proficient cat burglar, being very agile in spite of his lameness and he could wriggle his way between bars 15cm apart. He also developed ways of disguising himself using a variety of clothes and making up his face with cosmetics. He also developed a method of altering his face such that he could not be recognised even by his family.

On 11th August, 1859 he entered a lady's house in Manchester, taking a large number of items which he concealed in a hole in a field. The police were aware of this ruse and kept watch on the field. Charlie turned up with another man to recover his winnings when the police pounced on him. He nearly killed the arresting officer and the other policemen arrested him. His mother came from Sheffield and swore that her son was with her at the time of the robbery. This act of perjury did not go down well with the court and Charlie was sentenced to six years penal servitude.

On his release in 1864 matters did not go well in Sheffield and he returned to Manchester and two years later he was arrested after being caught entering a house at Lower Broughton. He was the worse for drink having consumed a quantity of whisky. He went down again this time for eight years penal servitude. He vowed never again to attempt theft under the influence of alcohol. He was sent to Wakefield Prison where he attempted to escape using a ladder he had stolen from some works at the prison. He had made a saw from tin which he used to cut a hole in the ceiling of his cell and he tried to climb onto the roof when a warder caught him. The warder tried to seize the ladder but Charlie forced the ladder down knocking the warder to the floor. Charlie ran along the wall of the prison, loose bricks caused him to slide off the roof and fall into the governor's residence. Charlie served his time in prisons at Millbank, Chatham and Gibraltar before his release in 1872. He was flogged at Chatham for taking part in a mutiny.

He changed his name to John Ward when he relocated his family to Darnall, a village near Sheffield. He carried on with his burglaries but his downfall was due to a woman, Catherine Dyson, a near neighbour, with whom Charlie became infatuated. She went along with him but the affair went sour when he became too insistent and she rejected him. In his anger, Charlie started to shout at her and her husband in public including brandishing a gun at them. A warrant was issued for Charlie's arrest. The Dysons relocated to Banner Cross, Eccleshall, Sheffield and Charlie continued with his thieving.

In 1876, he was confronted by a Police Officer whilst entering a house at Whalley Range near Manchester. Charlie shot the Policeman who subsequently died. A young man named William Habron was arrested having had a confrontation with the late Police Officer. William was found guilty but he was too young at 18 years of age to hang and he was sentenced to life imprisonment. Charlie had watched the proceedings of the court from the public gallery.

Charlie then visited the home of the Dysons' residence and he brandished a gun in front of Catherine. Her screams summoned her husband to the door whereupon Charlie shot him dead. Wanted notices appeared countrywide offering a reward of £100 for Charlie. He then went on an orgy of burglaries visiting numerous places including Nottingham and Derby.

In early 1877 he lodged opposite the Midland Station in Derby in order to appraise himself of the premises of an outfitters shop. He returned later to Derby and visited the outfitter's shop on London Road close to the Derwent Hotel, which was owned by John Arthur Wailer. Charlie confessed to stealing 17 women's mantles or jackets worth £5.25 each as well as £20 in cash.

He then went to Nottingham and acquired a mistress named Susan Bailey taking a house in the Broad Marsh area, very bad slums at that time. They called themselves Mr and Mrs Thompson. One night the police arrived at the house when they were both in bed. Charlie asked the police to vacate the room whilst he dressed himself and he escaped through the window.

He then turned up in London with wife and mistress. He burgled a house at Blackheath and as he was leaving with his spoils, he was met by Police Officers. He shot one of the officers in the arm and was promptly arrested. The police did not realise who they had arrested, the charge being the attempted murder of a Police Officer. His name on the charge sheet was John Ward. Later his mistress Susan, recognised him as the 'Gentleman Burglar' the much sought after, Charles Peace.

On his way back to Sheffield Charlie leapt from the train and one of his escorts caught him by the shoe. He suffered an injury in the foot. One cannot help considering how Charlie would have prospered if he had used his many talents and skills in legal pursuits. He was gifted more than most and a man who could overcome so many disabilities could overcome any problems that life might throw at him. So why did he pursue the life like the one he led? The only answer which springs to mind is a love of risk, the love of the chase, an easy way to become rich? We shall never know the truth.

On 4th February, 1879 the trial of Charles Peace started at Leeds Crown Court. He was hung on 25th February, 1879, 21 days after the commencement of his trial. He languished in Armley Prison, Leeds between times.

The result was that he became a folk hero and his name is still quoted as substitute for the 'bogey man'.

It would appear that the only person he respected and liked was the Reverend John Henry Littlewood, who was originally from Barlow,

Derbyshire. Charlie first met him at Wakefield prison when he was the Assistant Chaplain. A genuine friendship was established and Charlie admired the man and trusted him. Whilst waiting for his execution Charlie was visited by the Reverend Littlewood and told him that 'I do want, as far as I can, to atone in some measure for the past by telling all I know to someone in whom I have confidence'. Charlie made a full confession and as a consequence, William Habron was released from prison.

A brave policeman

This short story honours the memory of a brave policeman who set out to deliver a thief and died in the process.

A girl, whom we only know as Sylvia, aged 17, of Riber, a hamlet within the township of Matlock, later admitted that she had stolen £2.47 in cash. P.C. Arthur Wright had custody of her when taking her to the Matlock Police Station pending her appearance before the magistrates. They were crossing the Hall Leys Park in Matlock when Sylvia broke free. She ran towards the river Derwent jumping into the cold and fast flowing river with P.C. Arthur Wright in hot pursuit. He too jumped into the river to save her but both drowned, When one looks at this river in March it is fast flowing and numbingly cold and no-one could survive in it for long.

The police officer was born at Apperknowle near Unstone and he was buried at nearby Dronfield on Thursday, 30th March, 1911.

Memorial to Police Constable Samuel Marshall

He is remembered in Matlock by a memorial stone provided by voluntary subscription to his memory in Hall Leys Park, near to where he jumped into the river.

Revolution and Mayhem

The Pentrich Revolution
The years following the defeat of Napoleon at the Battle of Waterloo in 1815 were troublesome times. There was much admiration of the French with their new freedoms and laws, placing them at least fifty years ahead of us. The prosperity brought with the war had then turned into unemployment and all that went with it. There were several small insurrections throughout the country with most of them happening in the newly industrialising areas of the North. People were starving and the Luddites, a band of English craftsmen and labourers who felt their livelihoods threatened by machinery and set about its destruction, were active. The major event, the 'Pentrich Revolution', took place in Derbyshire and Nottinghamshire, with emphasis on the former.

This unhappy event failed through lack of discipline and good leadership. Four men were the instigators: Jeremiah Brandreth a framework knitter (stockinger), Isaac Ludlam a stone getter, William Turner a stonemason and George Weightman. Brandreth was from Sutton-in-Ashfield, Nottinghamshire and the other three were from South Wingfield, Derbyshire.

Brandreth used the White Horse Inn at Pentrich to instigate a revolution. The parlour was soon full and men kept calling and leaving, whilst Brandreth was dishing out orders, promising them all that he would lead them to bread, beef and beer. He was known as the Nottingham Captain and he produced a map showing the route they would take to Westminster where they would petition Parliament for better wages. He promised £100 cash to each participant as well as a pound of bread, a pint of spirits and a quart of ale. From Nottingham they would then progress to London being joined by thousands more men to support their cause. On arrival in London he planned they would create a Parliament with further promises of more food and better wages.

They assembled and set forth walking overnight from Pentrich on 9th June, 1817. They had planned on having two barrels of gunpowder hidden in a barn at Heage and forty pikes hidden in a quarry near Pentrich. They had already cast some lead bullets and they intended to take lead off church roofs if needed. Their initial aim was to take over the Butterley ironworks where they could then manufacture all manner of weapons.

However, there was a government agent amongst them named Oliver who was sending messages out to his masters. The conspirators were unaware of this man's real purpose.

On arrival at the Butterley Foundry, the gate keeper refused them entry and the workmen wanted nothing to do with the marchers. The whole venture went astray from then on. Whilst some more men joined the marchers many also deserted. They made their way towards Ripley hoping for more men to join their venture. They arrived at Codnor and went into the Glass House Inn and drank it dry. They then progressed to the nearby French Horn Inn and finally to the Junction Navigation Inn at Langley Mill overlooking the canal basin, where the same happened. They were now in Nottinghamshire and Oliver was still sending messages back to his employers.

They pressed on to Eastwood and their next target was Kimberley prior to advancing on Nottingham. They did not make it. They arrived at a hamlet called Giltbrook where they were to meet the end of their escapade. Eighteen mounted soldiers – the 15th Regiment of the Light Dragoons – appeared in the distance, which had an electrifying effect on the marchers as they started to run away as fast as they could. The revolution was over.

The death of Jeremiah Brandreth

The trials of the captured conspirators opened at Derby on 15th October, 1817. The three chief conspirators were sentenced to death by hanging, drawing and quartering, the last time this sentence was passed in England. This was commuted to hanging and beheading. The rest of the prisoners were either sent to Australia or pardoned.

Footnote: The Glass House Inn was rebuilt many years ago and is now an Italian restaurant, the French Horn Inn was rebuilt but retained its name, the Junction Navigation Inn is much as it was at the time but renamed the Great Northern Public House. The area where the rout took place at Giltbrook is now under the new IKEA store. The block on which they were beheaded is in the Derby Museum. The then Duke of Devonshire who owned the village of Pentrich had the dwellings which housed any of the conspirators pulled down. The sites are now occupied by new houses which have commemorative plates telling us who lived there in 1817.

A scholarly and detailed book about this event *England's Last Revolution, Pentrich 1817* by John Stephens (ISBN 0 903485 43 5), now long out of print, can be loaned from the Inter Library Loan Service through your own local library.

Reform Act riots

Many had anticipated the benefits of the Reform Act, therefore people eagerly awaited the outcome from Parliament when the 1831 Act was being debated. The House of Commons had passed the Bill thus giving more people the right to vote but the House of Lords had rejected it. The people were not only disappointed but angry. Derby's first knowledge of this outcome came with the coach from London which arrived at seven o'clock on Saturday evening 8th October, 1831. Some people had assembled to hear the news and they decided to mark the death of the Bill by sounding the bell of All Saints Church having forced the vicar to hand over the keys. Very soon the bells in the other churches in Derby had taken up the chorus; All Saints, Saint Alkmunds and Saint Peters. It was a ragged performance but an enthusiastic one.

By ten o'clock in the evening a number of persons had assembled in the Market Place in a state of considerable excitement. William Bemrose who had a shop in the Cornmarket was an outspoken critic of the Reform Bill and was singled out as a target for the mob. Bemrose sold books, music and musical instruments. He had an apprentice named Henry Morley who was to give evidence of the attack. Henry saw the crowd in the Market Place and Cornmarket and he warned Mrs Bemrose, whose husband was away. He also told her that the mob was advancing on the shop and would attack it. The mob arrived to find the ground floor windows shuttered so they attacked the upstairs windows with stones until most of them were shattered. They went away but returned in the early hours of the following morning, breaking the remaining windows and the shop sign. They returned at three o'clock in the morning and made holes in the shutters using iron bars. Henry could see men's arms coming through the holes grabbing anything within reach. An hour or so later they returned yet again and broke down the shop door completing their ravaging by the breaking of the window shutters. About twenty of the rioters entered the shop and started throwing books, paper and musical instruments about. Some carried some of the spoils outside, others threw them through the window and onto the street. Rioters passing by either carried the goods off or kicked them about. Boys ripped the pages out of the books and threw them into the air in handfuls. As dawn broke they went away, but one man threatened Henry Morley that they would return at night and 'finish him up'.

One can imagine the terror of the situation for Mrs Bemrose and Henry Morley, trapped as they were and at the mercy of an angry mob. The full devastation was apparent on the Sunday morning. Other premises had been attacked due to the owners' being in favour of the Reform Bill. A short list would include Thomas Cox's house in Friargate, Markeaton Hall owned by the Mundy family, Chaddesden Hall owned by Henry Sacheverell Wilmot where a dwelling house, stable, coach house and outhouses were demolished. In the town street lamps and windows were broken and shops were looted. Some rioters were arrested and taken to the Gaol.

The Mayor, Town Council and law abiding citizens were in a state of fear and panic. The Mayor called a public meeting for nine o'clock on the morning of Sunday, 9th October at the Town Hall in the Market Place. He wanted to see what could be done to stop the riots. Some of the rioters demanded that three people arrested and jailed the night before be released. The rioters told the Mayor that they could break open the prison, which they promptly did. A crowd of about fifteen hundred marched to the Gaol on Friargate. They were carrying a cast iron lamp post which they had uprooted. The turnkey, Ralph Wibberley, hearing the approach of the mob secured the outer door. Wibberley then advised the governor to accede to their demands. This was done and they released the prisoners who joined them and who were hoisted shoulder high with everyone cheering. They then broke down the doors of the jail using the battering ram and freed the other twenty-three prisoners.

The mob then targeted the County Gaol on Vernon Street, shouting as they went 'Reform' and 'to the County Gaol'. On arrival, the Governor appeared and told them to disperse, only to be answered with curses and a shower of stones. In response armed guards appeared on the prison wall. The Governor gave the order to fire and after several shots the rioters calmed down considerably. There was only one injury a John Garner, aged 17, was shot in the stomach. As it happened, this young man was playing no part in the riot. He died the next day.

As the Mayor had requested, a troop of the 15th Hussars from Nottingham Barracks arrived at about 5.30 on the Sunday afternoon. Their presence was enough to calm the situation. Along with Special Constables they patrolled the streets through the night. There were some looters and rioters still roaming the town.

On the morning of Monday 10th October, people were assembling again in the Market Place. Arrangements had been made for the people to sign a petition in favour of the Reform Act to be sent to the King. The stalls laid out for the signing were smashed up by the now smaller mob. The Magistrates decided somewhat belatedly, to step in. They read the Riot Act and asked the commander of the soldiers to clear the Market Place. After a long delay, the soldiers brandishing their sabres moved towards the rioters. They also carried loaded carbines (a light and short type of rifle). Those in the Market Place tried to leave but were hampered by the narrow streets, which were their only means of escape, and there were still more people arriving in the town.

The casualties started to mount. John Garner was the first, John Hickin was the second, shot by accident, the bullet had already made a hole in a Josiah Shepherd's hat. Henry Haden was third, killed by the crush of the crowd. They were all innocent bystanders. There is no record of the injuries sustained.

The situation calmed over the next few days. More Hussars started to arrive as already requested by the Mayor from Radbourne, Burton-on-Trent and Leicestershire and they assisted the troop of the 15th.

The consequence was that many thousands of pounds worth of damage had been done but the general consensus was that matters could have been worse. When Derby considered forming their own Police Force, the memories of these riots were at the forefront of their minds.

Nottingham, Derby's near neighbour, suffered worse damage. The Duke of Newcastle's town house was gutted by fire. This building is now the city's Art Gallery and Museum.

The Battle of Piesefield

Belper before the arrival of the cotton mills was known for its nail manufacture. This was a cottage industry and the men and some women were employed making nails for many different purposes. The men were strong in limb and stronger in temper and were quick to engage in any battles that occurred. The famous one was the Battle of Piesefield.

In 1837, the Midland Railway was being built through Belper, a huge undertaking due to a large excavation needed to sink the line to below ground level, which necessitated the building of a bridge for every road and lane that crossed it. Railway Navvies were hard men, as hard as the nailers. This mix of men had to lead to trouble.

Queen Victoria's accession to the throne took place at her coronation on 22nd June, 1837; a good reason if ever there was one to have a celebration. Some nailers had been employed on the line. The railway company provided beer enough for the navvies to have a celebration and to drink Her Majesty's health. The Belper navvies accused the original navvies of taking more than their fair share. They were however, outnumbered.

Some ran up Swinney Lane to recruit more of their number and this enlarged force swept down Swinney Lane and onto the railway works, some brandishing nailer's hammers. The navvies were forced to retreat and left the field clear for the nailers to consume the beer. No attempt was made to inform the Parish Constables. They could not have mustered enough constables to have any effect on the situation which by now had become out of control.

Much blood was shed that day and the navvies were only too happy to distance themselves from the nailers.

Prize fight

This form of bare knuckle boxing was illegal by 1851 and such contests had to be held at secret locations. These matches were popular with gentlemen gamblers. One such event was arranged on 16th December, 1851 at Cross o'th'Hands, West of Turnditch. The pugilists were Tom Paddock (the Redditch Rustic) of Redditch, Worcestershire and Harry Paulson (or Poulson) of Newark on Trent, Nottinghamshire, a Navvy Gang Gaffer. The spectators had occupied the inn nearest to the location for the match and having drunk their tipples they gathered at the site of the fight having armed themselves with cudgels taken from the inn comprising the legs from the tables, stools and chairs. The Parish Constable had heard of the event and set off to Belper for help.

Superintendent Constable William Wragg of Belper arrived with four magistrates, one of whom was Jedediah Strutt. The latter read the Riot Act and told the crowd to disperse quietly. Predictably they ignored him. Many bets had been placed and the punters wanted to see a finish to the match. Wragg tried to force a passage into the crowd aiming to arrest the pugilists. He was struck and kicked nearly senseless. Meanwhile the fight continued to its climax until Paulson was incapable of pursuing it and the victory was handed to Paddock after 95 minutes of pummelling each other.

The two boxers with their seconds and the referee set out for Derby. However news of their approach had been sent to the Derby Police who arrested them. They were transported to Belper by a special train for examination by the magistrates. Two of the ring leaders in the fray were transported from Coventry. As they approached the Police Office they had stones thrown at them, possibly by Paulson's supporters. Nine other men were charged with riot and the assault on Wragg.

At the Assizes on 16th March, 1852, the pugilists and three other men were each given ten months in prison, the referee four months and the rest of the detainees five months apiece.

This was not their first fight but a return fight. They had previously met at Sedgebrook, near Grantham, Lincolnshire.

High Treason and assassination

Anthony Babington

After Mary, Queen of Scots surrendered to Queen Elizabeth, she was held in confinement to the day when she was executed. She was kept at a variety of venues, all at a distance from London and one of these was Wingfield Manor, South Wingfield. Here she was under the care of the Earl of Shrewsbury who, along with other large houses, owned the Manor.

There is not enough space to cover the full details of her confinement, dealt with elsewhere by many biographies. Shrewsbury was an ideal jailer to act on behalf of Queen Elizabeth. He was loyal to the crown, had space for housing a captive and most of all he was rich. He had to be constantly vigilant of Mary's movements and hangers on. She was an ardent Catholic whilst Elizabeth was an ardent Protestant, and they were close relatives, Elizabeth being a daughter of Henry VIII and Mary the grand-daughter of Margaret Tudor, sister of Henry VIII.

A group of young Catholic men were in thrall to Mary and dreamed of putting her on the throne by usurping Elizabeth. A leader of this group was Anthony Babington, a Catholic squire of Dethick near Matlock. His income was £1,000 per annum, a sum that one could only dream about, worth at least £1,000,000 per annum today. He had exceptional charm and personality and he was gallant, adventurous and daring in defence of the Catholic faith.

He headed a group of men who were plotting to release Mary from her imprisonment and place her on the English throne. Mary's one time emissary wrote to her advising that Babington held a letter from Scotland and she had also received a second communication approving of Babington as a point of safe contact. His Derbyshire house was near to her prison. Mary wrote the first of many letters to Babington on 25th June, 1586 which was intercepted by Walsingham, Elizabeth's spy catcher. Babington's reply was feckless, 'I write unto her touching every particular of this plot'. He had signed his own fate! On 4th August, he was taken captive and thence to the Tower of London where he was held prisoner.

After her trial Mary was found guilty. She had no defence council, this was not allowed where treason was concerned. She was found guilty, the inevitable outcome of the whole affair. The trial was held in a room above the Great Hall at Fotheringhay Castle in Northamptonshire. Elizabeth had insisted that sentence should not be passed before she had time to consider the matter. The court met again after ten days when it reconvened in the Star Chamber, Westminster. Mary was found guilty and was condemned to die by beheading.

She was led to the scaffold where the executioner awaited her. The first blow missed her neck but cut into the back of her head, the second blow severed the head from the neck. It fell to the floor and her hair wig came off revealing her grey hair adding to the pathos of her death.

She was forty-five years of age. The irony of the situation was that on the death of Elizabeth, Mary's Protestant son James VI of Scotland acceded to the throne of England as King James I.

Babington and his plotters were also executed and their estates seized. His home at Dethick was slighted and there is nothing left to see apart from a lonely church. The farm at this location might retain elements of his big house. In recent time the farm was owned by Simon Groom of *Blue Peter* fame, which programme often used the farm as a location for filming.

The Phoenix Park murders, Dublin

Phoenix Park in Dublin is the largest public park in Europe at 709 hectares and boasts the tallest obelisk in Europe at 62 metres as well as a zoo.

A member of the Cavendish family who lived at Chatsworth House was appointed as the Chief Secretary for Ireland. Lord Frederick Cavendish was the brother of the 7th Duke of Devonshire. He arrived in Ireland to take up his post in 1882, within 24 hours of his arrival he was dead.

On 6th May, Cavendish along with the Permanent Secretary of Ireland, Thomas Henry Burke were walking in Phoenix Park, their destination being the Viceregal Lodge, the residence of Lord Spencer the Lord Lieutenant of Ireland. Suddenly both men were set upon and stabbed. Their attackers ran off. Someone ran into the lodge grounds shouting 'Lord Frederick Cavendish and Mr Burke are killed'. Doctor Thomas Myles of the Doctor Steven's Hospital rendered assistance to no avail. They had both bled to death.

The assailants were apprehended and taken into custody. They boasted that they were members of the Irish National Invincibles. They were tried along with three other conspirators and all five were hanged. The trial found that Lord Cavendish was not a target of the assassins but Burke was, the former being killed in error.

The political effect was considerable and affected Ireland deeply. Charles Stewart Parnell, an Irish Protestant landowner and a Home Rule Member of Parliament of Great Britain and Ireland, made a speech condemning the murders, which made him very popular in Ireland and Britain. Eventually, this was to affect the question of home rule which was delayed until the outbreak of the First World War when the bill was passed but delayed until after the war.

Cavendish's body was brought to Chatsworth by train to the Cavendish's private station at Rowsley, which can still be seen in the new Peak Shopping Village. The hearse carried the coffin to the church at Edensor on the estate. The route was lined with mourners on both sides of the road and over 30,000 people including 300 Members of Parliament followed the hearse. He was buried with his relatives in the churchyard on 11th May, 1882. He was the second son of the 7th Duke of Devonshire and was also the nephew of the then Prime Minister William Ewart Gladstone.

Murder

Murder in the frankpledge of Bontesal
'Henry, son of Richard of Bondesaal killed Ralph, son of Osbert with a knife in the vill. Of Bontesal, fled at once and is suspected. So he is to be exacted and outlawed. His chattels 2s 8d for which the Sheriff is to answer. He was in the frankpledge of Bontesal which does not have him now, so it is in mercy. William, son of Richard de Bondesaal, brother of Henry, absconded on account of the death, so his chattels are to be confiscated for the flight. His chattels 5s 4d for which the sheriff is to answer. William is come now and asked how he would acquit himself, denies the death and all and for good and ill puts himself on the country. The jury say that he is not guilty, so he is quit. But because he was present and did not arrest or pursue, he is in mercy. Walter de Ribuf the coroner did not attach Walter Bate, who took part in the aforesaid death, so to judgement in him.'

This document dated April, 1281 gives us an insight into justice at this time. This is the oldest document consulted for this book.

A Derbyshire Eyre or court had been summoned at Derby to look into the happening at Bonsall.

To help the reader the following words are converted to modern English: Bontesal, Bondesaal refers to Bonsall, a village west of Matlock, Frankpledge was a mutual surety that was a reciprocal promise, Eyre was a court of itinerant justices, a vill was a township.

Murder in a church
On New Years Day, 1422, a soldier was murdered in the Parish Church of St. Mary and All Saints, Chesterfield. Three men were implicated, Thomas and Richard Foljambe together with Thomas Cokke, the Chaplain, led an army of Lancastrians, two hundred strong into the church to attack all those present for reasons not known.

Henry Pierpoint was injured in the assault but William Bradshaw was struck and he fell to the ground close to the altar and such were his injuries that his brains spilled onto it. Pierpoint was sent home wounded. It was thirty years before the perpetrators were brought to justice.

Such behaviour at that time in a church was looked upon as being a serious act of sacrilege.

The Bakewell 'Tart'

Wendy Sewell, a legal secretary of Stoney Middleton was walking across Bakewell Cemetery when she was set upon and brutally murdered. The date was 12th September, 1973 and she was 32 years of age. A local youth, Stephen Downing aged 17 of Milford, north of Bakewell, was working as a gardener in the cemetery at the time and he became the prime suspect. He had notified the police about her bloodied body lying on the grass, naked from the waist down and part of her brassiere had been removed. She had been sexually assaulted and had been beaten about her head by a pick-axe handle. A witness had seen her enter the cemetery at approximately 12.30 p.m. She died on 14th September in Chesterfield Royal Hospital. She had been so brutally beaten that was unable to tell the police anything about her attacker.

Downing was arrested and after interrogation he signed a confession. He had a mental age of an 11 year old. He had told the Police that he had found her on the ground covered with blood and his explanation of why the blood was on his clothes was because he had shaken her head. He was taken to the Police Station in Bakewell where he was interrogated for nine hours. A statement was signed by Downing and there was no solicitor present!

The trial took place 13th-15th February, 1974 at Nottingham Crown Court. Downing pleaded not guilty.

Norman Lee, a Forensic Scientist, stated that the blood found on Downing could only have been on his clothes if he had been responsible for the murder. He was found guilty by a majority verdict. The judge sentenced him to be 'Detained at Her Majesty's pleasure' with the stipulation that he serve at least ten years. Detained at Her Majesty's Pleasure means indefinitely. He refused to admit to the crime which took away his eligibility for parole.

He was convicted of the crime and spent 27 years in prison before he was released. He owes this to the editor of the local newspaper, Don Hale who championed Stephen's cause for seven years and wrote a book about it. Don Hale's researches were handed to the police and a fresh enquiry was opened and when it closed the police stated that they were not looking elsewhere for a conviction. This is known as 'In Denial of Murder' also known as 'IDOM'.

Ten months after the case was closed and Downing found guilty a witness told that she had seen Downing leaving the cemetery at the same time as Wendy Sewell was walking to the rear of the cemetery chapel. A Court of Appeal dismissed this development on the grounds that the new witness was short sighted and trees grew such that they obscured the rear of the chapel. This 15 years old witness was interviewed and it became clear that she had given false information.

Stephen's parents made contact in 1994 with Don Hale who decided to investigate the case against Downing. Hale with Downings' parents started to campaign for a retrial for their son. His first task was to investigate Wendy Sewell's background. He found that she was sexually promiscuous and was known as the 'Bakewell Tart', a corruption of the famous Bakewell Pudding. Hale also investigated other murderers. The case was referred to the Criminal Cases Review Commission in 1997. In 2001 Downing was released after 27 years of incarceration. This attracted media interest world wide as this was as far as was known the longest miscarriage of justice in Britain.

A fresh appeal was mounted on 15, January, 2002 to determine Downing's guilt or otherwise. The counsel for the Crown accepted the defence's arguments:

Downing's confession should not have been given to the jury. He had been questioned for eight hours when the police shook him and pulled his hair to keep him awake. He had not been cautioned to the effect that what he said might be used in evidence against him.

The Crown agreed with the defence's argument that modern forensics would have come up with a different opinion of the blood splatter at the scene.

The Right Honourable the Lord Justice Pill advised the court that they were not to judge the guilt of Downing but to consider whether the conviction was safe or not. The court decided that the confessions were unreliable and Downing's conviction was quashed. The Derbyshire Police revealed that the findings of a new investigation after interviewing 1,600 witnesses had cost £500,000. Downing refused to be interviewed again. The Police could not find anyone else who might have been connected with the murder and they had to find the case closed.

Downing remains the prime suspect and the Police could not submit the results of their new enquiry under the 'double jeopardy' rule. It would require new evidence to place Downing on trial again. Don Hale in his book 'Town Without Pity' named some possible suspects. These names cannot be revealed as a court case is pending.

Substantial damages were paid to Downing as he had not been told that he was under arrest and had been denied a solicitor.

Interim payment of £250.000
A final payment of £500,000

Downing's imprisonment was traumatic as he was forced to change prisons eight times. He suffered assault by his fellow inmates for his alleged sex offences. He was in Littlehey Prison, Cambridgeshire when he was released. On release he could not find anyone to employ him.

Don Hale was once a professional football player with Bury Football Club and Blackburn Rovers until an injury forced him out of the game. He had a spell with the BBC writing features and became editor of the Matlock Mercury in 1985. Whilst investigating the Downing's case he was attacked on the streets and a car just missed knocking him over. He was named the Journalist of the Year (2001) by *What the Papers Say*, and was *The Observer's* Man of the Year (2001) as well as being awarded the OBE (2002). This story will run for many years yet.

In 2008, Downing admitted that he was obsessed with the idea of becoming a policeman. He acquired many items of police uniform from advertisers on the web. This is only legal when all the insignia is removed from the apparel. Downing set himself up with what looked like a police uniform and presented himself in the Aldi Store on Station Road, Buxton where he attempted to buy four packs of shandy. The check out assistant refused to serve him assuming him to be a policeman in uniform. This was reported to the police who arrested him. He also sported a badge having 'Photographix' on it, his trading name as a photographer.

He was wearing dark clothing with a check strip attached and a badge which stated 'Derbyshire Constabulary Armed Response Vehicle Unit'. He was brought before the court on the charge of impersonating a Police Officer. He was fined £437 with £650 costs and a victim surcharge of £15.

Pottery Cottage

Road blocks were set up near Chesterfield in January, 1977 in an attempt to waylay Billy Hughes who had escaped custody and was armed and had a background of violence. The police were asking people to search outhouses and any place which could hide a criminal.

He was en route from a court hearing to Leicester Jail when he stabbed a police officer and manacled his victim to another officer. He took control of a taxi and its driver before continuing on foot. In spite of the police searching on foot and by helicopter no trace could be found of him.

Little did the authorities know that he had detained some people at Pottery Cottage on Eastmoor near Baslow. They were Gill and Richard Moran, their daughter Sarah aged ten, and grandparents Arthur and Amy

Minton. He allowed Amy Minton to walk the dog and let Arthur and Amy Minton go to Chesterfield and forced Arthur to take money from his office. Those who were left at the cottage were held as hostages and Hughes threatened that if the Mintons tipped anyone off about what was happening he would kill the Morans. However Richard, Sarah and the Mintons were murdered and Gill was taken as a hostage.

When the police approached the cottage, Hughes made a run for it with Gill as a hostage using one of the family cars. He did not get far, as he ran into a road block on the Buxton to Macclesfield road. Using Gill as a foil threatened to kill her with a gun and an axe, he demanded a get-away car. He grew frustrated with the negotiations and made off to Rainow whereupon a marksman shot him dead. We cannot begin to imagine how Gill suffered the ordeal and the loss of her family. This was the worse crime ever recorded in Derbyshire. Mercifully she was not asked to give evidence at the inquest.

Gill Moran lived in Paris for a while with her sister and later she married and had a baby which she named Jayne Sarah, her murdered daughter's name. Hughes's wife Jean moved to Blackpool where she took her own life. The cottage, near to the Highwayman Inn was renamed and sold in 1978.

HM Inspector of Prisons was critical of the method of dealing with such prisoners and the police were criticised for not warning the prison about Hughes's violent nature.

The copy-cat murders

In a quiet lane leading from Eastmoor to Curbar three male corpses were found. Clod Hall Lane became the centre for the hunt of a murderer. The location had been attributed to the adjacent village of Baslow.

The murdered men were George Stobbs, aged 48, found in June 1960; his car was found abandoned in Baslow Lane. William Elliot, aged 60, found in March, 1961 who had been subjected to a violent attack; his bubble car was found abandoned in Chesterfield. The third person was never identified.

Later the Metropolitan Police were investigating similar murders in London: Norman Rickard aged 38 found in February, 1962, a bachelor and an Admiralty supply officer. He had been stripped and strangled with his hands tied behind his back and had been placed in a locked wardrobe in his basement flat where pictures of naked men posing as body builders adorned the walls.

A few days later, Alan Vigar aged 23 was found locked in a wardrobe in his flat. He also had been stripped and strangled. A party had taken place there with the party goers unaware that a dead body was in the flat. The alarm had been raised by a club hostess who had been invited to the party by a 'round faced man'.

The two police forces liaised in the belief that the two sets of 'copy cat' killings might be linked.

Michael Copeland, a soldier, became the prime suspect for the Clod Hall Lane murders. He had previously murdered a boy near to the barracks. He was tried at Birmingham Assizes and was sentenced to death but this was commuted to life imprisonment. There was no apparent connection with the London murders.

There have been numerous copy-cat murders the world over, a fair number of which have taken place in Great Britain.

'A Horrid and Inhuman Murder'

Thus a local paper blazoned this event and added the words 'and Robbery' for good measure.

On Wednesday, 16th July, 1823, a Mr William Wood, a respectable manufacturer of Eyam, was walking along the highway at Whaley Bridge in the company of a young woman. A shower of rain came and Mr Wood suggested that they shelter in a nearby quarry at Longside on the old road between Disley and Whaley Bridge. The woman declined and carried on walking.

This young woman had taken note of a gang of Irish mowers (hay cutters using scythes) numbering seven in total from which three detached themselves and went into the quarry. A few hours later Mr Wood's body, covered in hay, was found in the quarry, badly beaten and 'mangled' with his eyes almost out of their sockets. It was later revealed that he had been robbed of £70, which was a considerable sum in those days.

The three men were pursued toward Derby and when two miles short of the city, they made off towards Nottingham. One of them was covered in blood. The pursuit followed them in a post-chaise and four horses with the young woman and Constables Newton and King both of Derby on board.

This turned out to be a wild goose chase. At the Coroner's inquest held at the Cock Inn, Whaley Bridge, several people testified that three suspicious looking men had been seen on the highway heading towards Chapel-en-le-Frith. One witness saw the body shortly after the murder and reported that some loose rocks were covered in blood. Mr Wood's head was cut in several places and his death was occasioned by heavy blows at the back of his head causing pieces of his skull to penetrate the brain. This was confirmed by the surgeon in attendance who had examined the body thoroughly. The verdict was wilful murder by persons unknown.

Other witnesses testified that the three men had turned up in Macclesfield in shabby attire. They visited several inns and seemed to be able to spend much money. They then bought new clothes, and took the Telegraph coach towards Manchester. The three men arrived in the town. Their old clothes were examined and found to be covered in blood. This was enough evidence to cause the police to pursue the men, one was caught immediately and was taken to the New Bailey Prison. The other two were pursued by a constable.

The man now in prison hanged himself by rigging a noose from a pipe. The warder was too late to save him although he was still breathing a little. He was Charles Taylor, aged 17 and a native of Salford. He had been convicted twice before for felony. The coroner set his court up at the Dangerous Corner public house and a verdict of Felo da se (suicide) was returned. The other two culprits evaded justice.

A so called Murder Stone was erected at the site of the deed and can still be seen.

'A Bloody and Inhuman Murder'

A Matthew Cocklane (alias Coghlan) was executed on the Derby gallows on 21st March, 1776. He was paying the price for murdering a Mrs Mary Vickars in her home in Derby. A pamphlet along with his death bed confession was printed at the time.

'The Life, Tryal, Behaviour, Confession of the last dying words of Matthew Cocklane was being executed for the barbarous, cruel, bloody and inhuman murder of Mrs Mary Vickars at her house in Derby, which he perpetrated in the night betwixt Sunday, 18th and Monday, 19th December, 1774.'

His confession reads:

'I, Matthew Cocklane, am now in the thirty first Year of my age. Was born in the town of Carlow in the Kingdom of Ireland of creditable Parents. My father followed the trade of a Tanner.

I was sent to school at an early age but I gave little heed to instruction and when arrived at the age of nine or ten years, frequently absented myself from school for weeks together.

At the age of 13, I enlisted into the 33rd Regiment and continued in it for about ten years.'

(Matthew then settled in Derby, married, and worked in the iron and copper works; then he fell into bad company.)

'I having got acquainted with a young fellow, one George Foster, this young man advised me frequently to commit things repugnant to civil society. He begged me to go along with him and that I should not want for money.'

(Matthew knew a girl in Derby who had worked for a rich widow, Mrs Vickars. The girl told him that Mrs Vickars never kept more than one servant and always had a large sum of money in her house.)

Matthew Cocklane and George Foster made a plan to rob the old lady and fixed on Sunday night 18th December. George hung about watching the house, and Matthew met him after finishing work at the copper mills at midnight. Matthew had an iron bar with him, or as he called it in his story, 'an iron pin'. Matthew got in the house and then opened the front door to let in George.

'We immediately rushed upstairs. I told him to take off Mrs Vickars whilst I went and searched for the money. Mrs Vickars jumped out of bed with a great deal of vigour. I immediately knocked her down with the iron pin. This not stopping the noise that she made my companion immediately seized on her and got her down behind the door.'

(While George was keeping Mrs Vickars from shouting for help Matthew broke open a lid of the money chest in the bed room and took out several purses. Just then, Mrs Vickars's maid appeared at the doorway, having come down from her attic room to see what the noise was.)

'I told her to go upstairs or I would take her life that minute.'

That was later to prove a fatal mistake for Matthew, but it was an effective threat, for the maid ran back upstairs. However, this was not the only interruption. It was a week before Christmas and there were parties and celebrations taking place, late at night. The town band was returning from one of these and happened to pass the house just as the maid ran back upstairs.

'At that instant the Town Waits or Town music were passing Mrs Vickars' house. This alarmed me. I went downstairs, thinking that my companion had only stopped Mrs Vickars' mouth with a handkerchief.'

The two thieves went by different ways to Nun's Green, then on the outskirts of Derby, and found when they counted the money that they had about £300 between them.

'We then settled it for me to go to the Leek Road and he to Chester for Liverpool and to meet there. I did not know that Mrs Vickars was dead. The first information I had of it was from a handbill which was read in

Murder 77

my hearing at a Public House in Liverpool. On my companion's arrival. I asked him if it was true. He told me he believed she was dead but it did not signify, for he had three gold rings from her fingers.'

The two murderers then took ship to Ireland where they tried their hand at highway robbery which they bungled. George Foster was shot and died three days later, and Matthew Cocklane was captured and brought back to Derby to stand trial. He thought that he had a very good chance of getting off. No-one had seen him breaking into or leaving, Mrs Vickars's house on the night of the murder. He had not taken any jewellery which could be proved to have belonged to Mrs Vikars. The maid had not seen his face in the dark, and could not swear that she had recognised him as one of the robbers in her employer's house. But she had heard a voice saying, 'Go back upstairs or I'll take your life this minute'. And she testified that it was Matthew Cocklane's voice.

This was enough for the jury and Matthew was condemned to death. Later, of course, he confessed and told the whole story. He was hanged in Derby on 21st March 1776.

'He was taken out of the Gaol and put in the cart about a quarter past eleven o'clock. On his way to the gallows a person (who is said to be a preacher amongst the Methodists) got into the cart and read to him all the way. When he arrived at the tree he got out of the cart and the Reverend Mr Henry prayed for him for some time. The Under-Sheriff indulged in him nearly an hour and a half in his devotion, after which he seemed quite composed, got into the cart, fixed the rope and assisted the executioner in pulling the cap over his face; all this he did with greatest resolution. At half past one the cart was drawn away which launched him into a boundless eternity.'

He was gibbeted in Derby.

Note: The word 'boundless' in this context, eternity by definition is boundless.

Enoch Stone

On Derby Road, Chaddesden, just East of Derby a stone is set which has the initials 'E.S.' carved upon it. This has long been known as Enoch's Stone as it commemorated the murder nearby of one Enoch Stone of Spondon.

By all accounts he was a quiet and unassuming man who was a little lame and led the church choir for a time with his flute. He was a framework knitter by trade. This was the time when most churches had a band rather than an organ. Once, when practising carols for the coming festive season at the Homestead, at that time the home of Doctor James Cade the surgeon, someone wanted the key not to be sounded and instead of calling 'Sound the G. Enoch', much to every body's amusement, he shouted 'Sound your Enoch' after which it became 'Sound the Enoch'.

He was well liked by many, so who brutally killed Enoch on the turnpike near to the butter factory on the Summer's evening of 23th June, 1856 and why?

Because of his disability he was unable to gain regular employment. Occasionally he was a silk glove maker. He was poor so why would anybody wish to kill him? His murderer was never found and the motive remains a mystery.

On the night of his murder he had walked from Spondon to Derby to collect a hamper of clothes that his son, who was in service, had taken home for laundering. After collecting these Enoch stopped at a Derby inn for a pint of beer which he drank with some bread and cheese. He left the inn sober as testified by the innkeeper Mrs Garnett. He reached Chaddesden where he was seen by two men at eleven o'clock at night. Mrs Garnett, along with the two men and the murderer were the last people to see Enoch alive. At this time, he was on Cherry Tree Hill heading for Spondon. A publican, William Peat, some ten minutes later heard a cry of 'murder' but he ignored it believing it was a drunkard.

A few minutes later two men came across the dying Enoch who they assumed to be a drunkard in his cups, so they continued on their way. This was necessary when out at night in those times for fear of being waylaid by possible robbers. They did notice that his face had been blackened and they thought the whole business was a prank. The blackening was in fact blood which had also covered his parcel. Had these people sounded the alarm Enoch might have survived his ordeal.

It was at one in the morning, when keeper Davidson and coachman Edwin Lavender, both en route to Derby train station to collect their employer, noticed a hamper on the road with clothes strewn around it. They stopped to investigate and found Enoch still breathing but unconscious, he lay in a pool of blood with his skull split open. His boots were missing and his pockets had been turned out. The two men tried to make him comfortable away from the turnpike. Another passer-by went to fetch a doctor and to alert the village constable. Spondon had six constables at that time the chief of which was a Mr Wright.

Edwin Lavender stayed with Enoch and Davidson took the coach on to Derby train station to meet his employer. At the same time he notified the Derby police. Meanwhile Doctor Cade arrived at the scene and Enoch was taken to his home on a cart. Cade sat with Enoch until he died at six in the morning without gaining consciousness, he could not therefore help the police with their enquiries. An inquest was postponed twice to give the police time to find the murderer. The police had picked up two Irishmen seen sleeping on the Meadows that night together with a woman who had been found wandering. As the police could not find evidence against them they were released from custody.

Later a Thomas Jones of Birmingham swore that he had seen a tramp named David Hall on Cemetery Hill on the night of the murder. Hall who was also called Welsh Mick was a notoriously bad character. When he was seen carrying a pair of boots under his arm the police placed him in custody for two weeks until they proved that he had not been in Derby that night but at Bromsgrove Fair (Southwest of Birmingham). He was released.

A reward of £120 was offered by the Police for information leading to the apprehension of the culprit by a local magistrate, Sir Henry Wilmot of Chaddesden Hall and a further reward of £100 was offered by the government and £20 by the parishioners of Spondon. But to no avail. A motiveless murder is the most difficult to resolve. Today's Forensic science would have been of huge assistance. Two days after his demise he was buried in the Chapel Street Cemetery, Spondon.

On 21st July an inquest was finally held at the Malt Shovel Inn at Spondon and the verdict returned that Enoch Stone was wilfully murdered by a person or persons unknown.

This might have been the end of the matter with another murder passing into the annals of crime with a forgotten victim, except that someone chose to erect a small stone bearing the initials E.S. carved upon it. For some years during the twentieth century the stone was lost to view being buried in the roadside hedgerow. It was recovered and passed to Derby Museum for safe keeping whilst building took place. It was finally

The Enoch Stone on the corner of Oregon Way and Nottingham Road (S Watson)

erected near to the place where Enoch lost his life. He is also remembered by a road nearby named 'Enoch Stone Drive'. The stone is located at the corner of Oregan Way and Nottingham Road.

These memorials are called Murder Stones. There is one located where William Wood was killed, see 'A Horrid and Inhuman Murder'. With another one at Great Longstone. The one in the woods above the Via Gellia, Cromford near to Ruggs Hall is commonly referred to as a Murder Stone, it is in fact a lump of limestone rock stained by Iron Oxide! There is no record of a murder ever having taken place in this location.

Samuel Marshall of Repton

The Derby Mercury reported 'A most shocking murder was perpetrated on Saturday evening last, on Samuel Marshall, a baker of Repton.

He was upon his return with an empty bread-cart, having delivered his bread and cakes, etc. to several villages, and particularly Rolleston-on-Dove. The next day being Wakes Sunday at that village near to Burton on Trent. He had received cash, it is said, to the amount of six or seven pounds, and was making his way home when his career was suddenly ended by some villain or villains unknown.

He was found about seven o'clock by one William Mountford, a labouring man, of Ticknall, who was passing by and saw the unhappy youth lying on the ground near to the Navigation Bridge at Willington, and his body mangled in a frightful manner.

He had received a violent blow on the head, and so has a deep cut behind the left ear, which seems to have been done with a pen-knife or some sharp instrument. They had cut his throat in such a manner that a piece of his flesh hung down to his chin, but had not penetrated his windpipe. His pockets were turned out, the contents taken.

As soon as possible the neighbourhood was alarmed, the body removed to Repton, and a warrant, and a hue and cry issued by a worthy magistrate. Persons were despatched to search the most suspected places. Handbills were printed and dispersed (offering a reward of £40 over and above what is allowed by Act of Parliament), and every means used to bring the perpetrator of this inhuman deed to punishment. But, notwithstanding that several have been taken up on suspicion, yet after examination they have been discharged, nothing substantial appear to incriminate them.'

Later the paper also reported, 'On Thursday night, about ten o'clock, a young man named James Wheldon, of the village of Rolleston (on Dove), near Burton-on-Trent, was brought to the county gaol, charged on a violent suspicion of having committed the murder near Willington, on the body of Samuel Marshall, baker.

He that day, underwent an examination of about eight hours before Sir Robert Barditt (sic Burdett) Bart. One of His Majesty's Justices of the Peace, when a very minute enquiry was made, and that the strictest impartiality, and it appeared by many corroborating circumstances that the above young man might personally be suspected of perpetuating the horrid deed, he was committed for trial at the next Assizes.

One particular we must not omit, which is that a blacksmith's hammer was found near the spot it was perpetuated in, having, it is supposed, been the instrument used on the barbarous occasion, and had been thrown over the hedge immediately after the murder.

On discovery of his hammer, several persons were dispatched to Rolleston, and upon enquiry the blacksmith missed the hammer, and afterwards it came out on the oath of this man that he had lent the hammer to Wheldon several days previous to the murder. The circumstance the prisoner hotly denies, saying he never borrowed a hammer from him in all his life. There are several circumstances incriminating him but how far they may weigh in the views of a jury, time only can determine.'

Quote: 'James Wheldon, charged with the murder of young Marshall, baker of Repton, was acquitted after a hearing of nearly six hours.' There was not enough evidence to sentence him.

Note: the narrative from the Derby Mercury has been repeated verbatim as an example of the florid language used in newspapers of the time.

Samuel Marshall's slate tomb stone can be seen in Saint Wystan's Churchyard, Repton. The stone has a tree carved upon it having five branches, one of which has been cut off. This was done to indicate the death of James and to indicate the survival of his four brothers. A depiction of the murder weapon is also shown. Samuel's father died the following year.

The rag and bone man

This case was popularly known as the 'Brimington wallpaper murder'.

Alfred Gough, a hawker, was popular with children as he toted for rags and bones. At Brimington near Chesterfield, he was seen by a little girl, Eleanor Windle. She was picking blackberries on the road to Chesterfield and upon seeing the hawker she grew excited by the thought of gaining a small trinket from him, a small parasol or windmill that she coveted. At home her mother had kept a half penny for this purpose. She accompanied Gough back to Brimington to collect the coin and was never seen again alive by her friends. The two were seen by John Tinsley, a carrier and by Harriet Johnson who lived on the lane. Harriet did not like the look of the situation and she left her house in order to investigate.

She discovered that Gough was exposing himself to Eleanor. Harriet procured a broom handle but was too late to catch them so she went back home. A highway labourer, John Cook, came across Gough's handcart with no-one in attendance. He waited to see if the owner would turn up and after a while he gave this up and went mushroom collecting. On his return the handcart had gone. Later, a Sarah Cantrill saw Gough pushing his handcart. It came to her notice that there was a large object on the cart covered by rags and lying on a piece of wallpaper from a parasol. This would later link the murderer with his victim.

Gough stopped at a toll house where he bought a glass of ginger beer. While he was doing this Eleanor's father arrived. He enquired of Gough about his daughter's whereabouts. Gough's answers were unsatisfactory. Windle entered the Three Horse Shoes Inn at Brimington where he met and spoke to P.C. Wright about his daughter's disappearance. Gough, having followed, had a short conversation with the two men and proceeded towards Chesterfield. Prior to reaching this town, Gough met Thomas Holmes also known as 'Mansfield Tom'. Gough arrived in Chesterfield where he left his cart with Thomas Newbury, a dealer in rags. He spent that night in a lodging house called the Beehive. The next morning Eleanor's father set out in search of his daughter. Brown found tracks made by the handcart leading into Hooles Plantation which lay on a private road from Staveley to Barrow Hill. He found an onion bag and a little distance beyond this his daughters' body. She had been raped and strangled.

Gough was arrested and charged with murder. Strangely for a Derbyshire case the trial was held at Leicester. The defence was a weak one which did not impress the jury. He was sentenced to death. Gough had an interesting background. He had been a member of the Leeds Constabulary, a soldier in the 17th Foot and served in India. However, upon returning to a civilian life he took to being an itinerant vendor living in lodging houses.

On a very wet 21st November, 1881, he was hanged at the county Gaol. A large crowd of onlookers awaited the tolling of the bell which told them that Gough had died on the scaffold.

Bones in a cesspit

At the time this murder was referred to as the 'Cesspit Murder'.

An almost complete male human skeleton was found in a cesspit in Chesterfield on the 28th August, 1846. Cesspits, apart from receiving all the waste products from the house, bathroom as well as kitchen, were also dumping grounds for dead dogs and the spoils from robbers who were on the run from the law. A cesspit was a common device whereby all the waste, solid and wet, accumulated in a pit in the ground from whence the water would soak away leaving the half solid matter. The smell from such a pit was breathtaking and this was a summer's day. The pit was shared by George Bunting, a flour dealer of Chesterfield and Mr and Mrs Townsend his neighbours. The last time it had been emptied was some fourteen months previously, this was to have some bearing on what was to be revealed. George Bunting had set three men to do the nauseating job of emptying the pit using buckets and spreading the waste on a nearby field owned by him. The men who emptied the pit were Valentine Wall and Richard Ashley with Thomas Green doing the spreading.

When they had removed about thirty buckets full, a number of bones were seen. They assumed not unreasonably that they were of some animal. They delved further and found more bones which were obviously human in origin. Then they found some male clothing comprising the remnants of a coat, a pair of trousers and a hat. One had flesh clinging to it. Thomas found some clothing on the field which he must have thrown out. They were men's clothes and Thomas found a pair of stockings, braces and a neckerchief to which he added some ribs and leg bones with two garters attached, one red and the other white. The search for bones continued until they had almost a full skeleton.

Mr Bunting told of the finds to two friends, Mr Wyatt, a butcher and Dr Hugh Walker, a medical practitioner. They confirmed that the remains were of human origin and the discovery of a human skull confirmed this. There were very few bones missing, only a few small bones and some teeth. The doctor confirmed that the skeleton was that of a man. The skull had been dealt a blow with a bludgeon and to support this they examined a stave three feet long also found in the cesspit. The skull was badly damaged with three fractures, and the bone around the eye sockets was fragmented. There was a large wound at the base of the skull. They decided that the police should be called in.

Another man Thomas Cowley, told the police that he had not found any bones when he had emptied the pit fourteen months previously. This led the police to remember a missing person, who had vanished on 7th December, 1845. The man was George Collis aged twenty-six years at that time. They called on the mother of George, Marty Mawkes and his girl friend Ellen Berresford. They confirmed that the clothing discovered in the pit was George's. Ellen remembered that his garters were red and white and the handkerchief had been hemmed by her. Any doubt that this was an accident was dispelled, the police were looking for a murderer.

In the evening of the following day, Platts, a butcher, went to a public house opposite his shop. It was noted that he had a cut on his hand and he explained that he had caught it on a hook in his shop. A Mrs Bellamy dressed the wound and a man from a wedding party called over to Platts that he could swear that he had seen someone in his shop. Later on Platts called at the Old Angel where the landlady asked after his injured hand and was told the same story as before. He then said that he intended to go to Mansfield to enter a raffle for a watch. On the following evening, two brothers saw Platts, Morley and a third unknown person carrying a sack which appeared to be heavy given the number of times they had to stop for a rest. As it had come from the Shambles they assumed that the sack held some offal. Eventually they turned into Buntings yard where the cesspit was located.

A few days later, people were enquiring of John Platts the whereabouts of his partner. One man told his friends that he believed that the missing man had been murdered by Platts. He confronted Platts, demanding to

Likeness of John Platts, the Murderer of Geo. Collis. *(Platts's Shop as it appeared at this*

The Cesspit Murderer, John Platts

know the whereabouts of his partner, to be told that he had gone to Macclesfield or Manchester. John Platts was interviewed on the 3rd September by Inspector Charles Cotterill. His answers to their questions did not satisfy the police. The next day, the Police searched Platt's house. A watch was found and a pair of boots which they were convinced were from George Collis. Platts told them that the watch had been bought from a William Beaumont alias 'Lank Bill' a local criminal. Beaumont denied all knowledge of the watch. A watchmaker confirmed that he had sold the watch to George Collis and a boot maker confirmed that he had made the boots for the same man. The landlord and landlady of the Old Angel could not support Platts' alibi.

The trial was complicated by the absence of a murder weapon and conflicting arguments from the prosecution and defence councils. Finally the matter was left to the jury to decide. They did not even leave the courtroom. In a matter of minutes they found the defendant guilty of murder. The judge sentenced Platts to death with no expectation of a reprieve. He was hanged on All Fools Day, 1847. He swore that he would die a brave man. Four journalists present as observers agreed that he did. The hangman, Samuel Haywood had no faith in the long drop and the result was that Platts died of asphyxiation.

Footnote: Shambles were the buildings where cattle were slaughtered and often bought and sold. Killing methods were crude and the cattle shed blood in copious quantities. It was said of Chesterfield's Shambles that when in operation the blood flowed as high as ones ankles. They were messy and unsavoury places and one cannot imagine the smell they gave up, a mixture of blood, urine and faeces on a hot Summer's day.

Jealousy

Benjamin Hudson was a very jealous man, one of the most corrosive feelings endured by man. He was married to Eliza, who had been a 'bit of a lass' in her time. She had two children by her uncle and one child by a William Hibberd. Eliza became depressed by her husband's manner and she left him to live with her father at West Handley, near to Clay Cross. On 24th April, 1873, Hudson started to pester her from outside a house where she was doing some cleaning. She did not know that he had borrowed a gun two days earlier from a John Morton. Eliza asked a friend Elizabeth Cole to walk with her as she went home and after going into a field her companion left her to her to make her own way home.

A little later George Gosling saw Benjamin looking 'shifty' and later George saw a body from a stile, which on closer examination tuned out to be Eliza facing face down and bleeding badly from her skull. It appeared that the skull was fractured as were some ribs and there were two teeth buried in the ground. She died some thirty minutes later. Benjamin was present and he too was covered with blood. He said out aloud that he had 'done for her' and 'I've ended it'.

At his trial his defence claimed that his client had acted in self defence, that it was a spur of the moment act and a crime of passion. The jury found him guilty of murder and the judge sent him to the gallows.

Suicide, matricide, patricide and infanticide

Suicide

Mather's Grave
This 'grave' is indicated on Ordnance Survey maps as Mathergrave, the local parochial name, at a cross roads. There is more than one version of the story about Samuel Mather.

Version one: As was customary for suicides, he was buried at a cross roads. At these cross roads there are several stones built into a dry stone wall, one of which bears the initials S. M. and is attributed to a Samuel Mather, another bears the date 1643 which is a mystery. He died in 1716, supposedly! The story behind this is that Samuel Mather cut his wife's throat and afterwards he cut his own throat. As the custom dictated Mather was duly buried at the cross roads in question. The Parish Records for Morton tell us that Samuel had fathered an illegitimate daughter in 1716 and she became chargeable to the parish rates of Brackenfield.

Version Two: It is said that Samuel took his own life in a barn so as to avoid the scandal of his daughter's birth.

The story becomes outrageous. It was also said that Samuel was drawn to his grave by two bullocks and when the animals rested a raven flew down to stand on the corpse. An ill omen in folklore. His stone and skeleton were relocated when the road was widened many years ago. The stones can be seen today built into the roadside wall, his skeleton was found at this time and it was reinterred under the largest stone. This ritual supposedly denies the victim his salvation!

In 1838, Thomas Bagshawe of Hazlebadge near to Bradwell had a similar fate except, one hopes without the raven.

Sometimes the victim had a stake driven through his heart. Another

Mather's Grave or what's left of it

fatuous ceremony was introduced later. The corpse had to be removed from the Coroner's Court after the case had been dealt with and it had to be buried within the following twenty-four hours and between 9 pm and midnight.

A curious poisoning at the Snake Inn

The Snake Inn sits on a steep hillside on the Glossop to Sheffield Road, the A57. This road from the Derwent Dams to Glossop curves in all directions as might a snake, hence its name.

An unknown fashionably dressed man booked into the inn at between 8.00 pm and 9.00 pm and enquired of the publican, Mr Rowarth, if he could have a bed for the night. He did not give his name or address. It transpired that he was heading towards Sheffield. He then ordered a glass of beer. He paid for all this before occupying his room. Later on the stranger treated the staff to two or three quarts of beer. He retired to his bed at about 11.00 pm and asked to be roused at 11.00 am the following morning.

At the time the publican knocked on his door with no response. Rowarth forced the door to be greeted by a strange sight. The comatose stranger lay on his bed, hardly breathing. He was unable to speak when addressed. On a table stood a half-pint spirits bottle, which contained a little laudanum but had contained much more. A water glass was near to the bottle which had obviously been used for drinking the poison. All those present at the inn tried to administer an emetic to no avail, the man died at about 1.00 pm. His apparel was examined and all that could be found was a handkerchief, a few matches and a little tobacco. He was 5 feet 8 inches tall, with a pale complexion, brown eyes, dark brown hair, sandy whiskers, a moustache, bald from his forehead to the crown of his skull, and he had a scar on his left elbow and many scars on his right knee.

He was attired in a suit of almost new pale blue serge (fashionable at that time), black felt hat with 'Lewis of Manchester' inside, grey knitted woollen drawers, black silk down vest, swansdown shirt, dark blue socks and light laced boots. All of this suggests a man of substance.

An inquest sat but adjourned.

Was this a carefully staged murder or suicide? The two possibilities could be argued forever, given what little evidence there was. There was no money on the man, but earlier he had paid for his room along with drinks, or did he spend until the money ran out? There was no suicide note.

Perhaps we shall never know the truth.

Attempted suicide and murder

Mrs Sarah Towle of the Coffee House, Little Eaton was found on her bed in the upstairs bedroom and she was dead. She was lying on her back with her left hand under her and with a severe wound to her throat.

Police Constable Ashton was summoned to the scene by William Pidcock of the nearby Anchor Inn. Her elderly husband said that at about midnight his wife had come to the bedroom and offered him some tea. This he refused. He was not alarmed by his wife's appearance and he went to sleep again. He awoke from his sleep with a sensation about the back of his neck, as if it had been scratched with a pin. He felt the area and found that he was wounded and bleeding. His wife lying to his side made a noise and on examination the husband found that she too had a wounded neck. As he left the room his wife said 'Oh William'. He made haste to Mr Pidcock and told him what had happened.

P. C. Ashton commandeered a trap and drove the old man to Duffield to see Dr. Hoskin's assistant who attended to the wound which whilst nasty was not life threatening. Hoskin's assistant accompanied the trap back to Little Eaton and examined Mrs Toole. A razor covered with blood was found near her body.

Later it was established that Towle's account of the happenings was a correct one. It became clear that on the previous night, Mrs Towle had tried to poison her husband. She had tried to encourage her husband to take a drink from a certain cup. He declined the offer and went to bed. After analysis the contents of the cup contained a strong poison. The conclusion drawn was that she had tried and failed to poison her husband and attempted to cut his throat later.

Abortions and Infanticide

A Woman in the Pillory

On 15th August, 1732, Eleanor Beare, wife of Ebenezer Beare a labourer of Derby was convicted of Procuring Abortions in women. Also it transpired that she had persuaded a man to poison his wife after they had quarrelled. The man decided to dig a hole and bury the poison instead of administering it.

The judge who tried her was greatly moved when summing up the evidence and giving his charge to the jury. He declared that 'he never met with a case so barbarous and unnatural'. Eleanor was sentenced to 'close imprisonment for a term of three years and to stand in and upon the pillory on the two next market days in the town of Derby'.

She was exposed on the pillory three days later, being the next market day. She was pelted with rotten eggs and any filth the onlookers could collect. Struggling violently she disengaged herself and jumped into the crowd. The Sheriff's Officers had difficulty in rescuing her.

She was brought out on the next week and was pilloried again. As soon as she mounted the platform, she knelt down and begged for mercy. The executioner noticed that she was struggling to get her head through the hole provided. The executioner pulled at her head dress and found concealed in it a large pewter plate, beaten out to fit the shape of her head. She threw it amongst the spectators. As soon as she was fixed a shower of eggs, potatoes, turnips and other vegetables were aimed at her from all directions. It was thought that she would not survive this bombardment. Having exhausted the root crops and eggs the crowd took to throwing stones instead. This caused so much wounding that blood streamed down the pillory.

The crowd relented at the sight of her and she was returned to the gaol looking very ill used.

Mary Spencer

Mary was the daughter of a James Spencer, grocer and farmer of Bonsall. Mary was twenty-six years of age and already had an illegitimate three year old daughter known as Adeline, commonly known as Addie. Her mother, Alice and her father had been aware for a while that Mary's behaviour was unusual for a young woman who normally had a happy disposition. She was also sleep walking. Her mother told her to join her sister in the latter's bed room. Mary then told her father that she was pregnant again. True to his Victorian mentality he told her to leave the house and to go away from the village. She left the house and wandered about Bonsall Moor with Addie. When milking his cows that same evening at about eight o'clock her father saw his daughter and Addie a field or two away.

Late on 4th July, 1880, Mary appeared at the door of her neighbour Elizabeth Spencer. Mary was in poor shape with her clothes bedraggled and soaking wet. After wandering about for a time, she had come upon a mere in one of her father's fields. She pressed her daughter close to her chest and lay in the mere in the hope that both of them would drown. Adeline did drown but this did not work for Mary as the water was too shallow. For two hours she tried desperately hard without success. She thought that drowning would be an easy death and it might have been had the water been deeper.

Suicide, Matricide, Patricide and Infanticide 91

Too afraid to go home she went to Elizabeth's house where the latter's husband Henry, along with Mary's father, went to the mere looking for Adeline. Henry found her body at the bottom of the mere and wrapped it in a shawl and brought her home. P.C. Hall, the village policeman, arrested Mary and took her to the lock-up in Wirksworth pending a trial at Derby Assizes. She was sentenced to death but this was commuted to life imprisonment.

Common in Derby

Infanticide was rife for many centuries but the Derby Assize Court took a lenient approach to this one time crime. The mothers were rarely sentenced to death; life imprisonment was used as an alternative.

In 1754, Mary Dilkes was found guilty of leaving her 'bastard' child on a sand bank on an island in the river Derwent in Derby known as the Holmes. She was executed, the first such for over twenty years.

In 1796, Susannah Moreton was sentenced to death along with a seventy year old man, James Preston. The charge was the murder of a baby. They were both sentenced to death. He was executed but Susannah was reprieved a minute before she was due to be hung with him.

At the Derby Assizes of March, 1822, Hannah Halley was convicted of causing the death of her baby by placing it in scalding hot water. She was employed at the Darley Abbey Mills at the time. She told the court that the devil had impelled her to kill her baby.

Hannah Slack was acquitted of infanticide in 1844, even when it was said that the doctor had certified that the child had died of arsenic poisoning.

In 1850, Elizabeth Vicars found that a tape had been tied round her baby's neck. She was found guilty for concealing a birth and was sentenced to a year in prison.

Patricide

The water cure

This event is often irreverently known as the 'Potty Murder'.

The Reverend Julius Benn had a son whose mental health was a cause for concern. He decided to try hydrotherapy, the then current rage for the cure of most illnesses, Matlock being the capital of this industry. The Reverend with his son arrived there in February, 1883 and booked lodgings at Hartley House at the bottom of the Steep Turnpike in Matlock. The Reverend was 56 years of age at the time and the son, William Rutherford Benn was 28.

They seemed to have settled in but six days after their arrival they failed to turn up for their breakfasts. George Marchant, the owner of the establishment went to morning service as he always did on Sunday mornings and on returning home the lodgers had still not appeared. George decided to investigate and upon opening the door to the visitor's room he saw blood spread everywhere. The Reverend was dead and a chamber pot lay nearby; it was evident that he had been struck on his head several times. William was in profound shock and had attempted suicide by cutting his own throat; his blood added to the carnage. William had suffered a total mental breakdown and was considered unfit to plead. However, he did admit killing his father using the chamber pot as a weapon.

William recovered with help from his family and he settled into domestic life. He married and his wife gave birth to a daughter, Margaret. Three years later, William's wife Florence died and this acted as a trigger whereby William's health broke down, this time permanently. He spent the next twenty-two years of his life in the Bethlehem Hospital, London and a further twenty-two years at Broadmoor Hospital, Crowthorne, Berkshire where he died.

Hartley House, Matlock

Margaret was raised by her relatives and changed her name to Rutherford. She grew up to become one of the nation's treasures as an actress. William Benn had a nephew who made his name as a politician as did his father who was elevated to the House of Lords as Lord Stangate. The latter's son is Anthony Neil Wedgwood Benn, recently the Member of Parliament for Chesterfield, some fifteen miles from the murder scene. Anthony renounced his title under the Peerage Act, 1963 enacted for him as his desire was to be a Member of Parliament. Margaret Rutherford was happily married to Stringer Davis who often appeared with her in her films.

This murder has much in common with another almost identical event, when the artist Richard Dadd was sent to Broadmoor for life for the murder of his clergyman father.

George Hobbs

George Edward Hobbs, aged 20 years, had been a pony driver at the Hornesthorpe Colliery until he had an accident which crippled him in one foot. Eventually he received compensation for his injury, the princely sum of £100. It was agreed with his mother that he would pay an agreed sum for his board and lodging. He then went on to spend the rest on alcohol.

George was of a large family. Apart from his mother Joanna and his father John William, a joiner, there were eight children, four boys and four girls, of which George was the eldest.

On Wednesday, 17th July, 1901, his father had taken advantage of a fine Summer's day to watch a game of cricket. George was not at home either. George turned up demanding his tea and when his mother told him it would be ready shortly George shouted 'Where's my father and who's the boss of this house?' His mother told him that his father was and always would be the boss of the house. George hobbled into the back yard declaring that he would take anyone on, shouting, 'I'll be the boss of the house and will show you something before tonight'. George re-entered the house demanding to know if his father had arrived home yet. He had not and George went upstairs and quickly came down again and out into the back yard, repeating the threats already made. Mrs Hobbs then saw George standing in front of the house brandishing a revolver before walking to the Bird in Hand public house. Joanna went to the door and her daughter Annie Maria tailed George to keep an eye on him. His brother Albert, saw George enter the Bird in Hand and ran back home to tell his mother and told his sister Annie Maria where George had gone. Albert ran across some fields to find his father. He told his father about George's behaviour. They both then went to the Bird in Hand. On seeing his father, George brandished the revolver and shouted, 'I've been an infidel all my life and I will be one when I die. Either I put a bullet into you, or me'. His father thought he was bluffing and he said that the revolver was not loaded. George's response was to fire the revolver into the sky, there was a loud bang. Bravely, John walked towards George with the intention of relieving him of the weapon. He grabbed at the weapon and they both fell to the ground. Suddenly, a further shot rang out and John fell to the ground wounded. They both climbed to their feet and it was evident that John was badly wounded. He made towards the Bird in Hand but before he got there, he fell to the ground crying, 'For Heaven's sake Georgie – his nick-name for George – don't shoot again I am half dead now'. Unmoved, George aimed the revolver and shot his father again. A bullet struck John in the thigh and as he fell to the ground George aimed the revolver at his father again saying, 'I'll finish you in less than five minutes'. Albert ran towards George and struck him over the head with a parasol. George fell to the ground along with his brother. George scrambled to his knees and fired again damaging his brother's fingers. The noise alerted the customers in the Bird in Hand who came out to see what the noise was about. They carried the two wounded men into the building and to safety. Annie Maria begged George to stop and his reply was a shot from his revolver which hit her near the right elbow. A second shot missed her.

The shots had been heard by a butcher, Leonard Gregory. He left his shop to find George shouting, 'I've done it!' George turned towards Gregory but before he could aim and fire, the gun was knocked out of his hand by a passer-by, Benjamin Jones. George was taken to the Police Station and was handed over to the police. He was charged with attempted murder.

The three members of the family who had been wounded were taken to the Chesterfield Royal Infirmary. Annie Maria was sent home as her wounds were superficial. Albert had to have an operation on his hand, and lost one finger. Mr Hobbs had two serious wounds, one to the right of his chest under the fourth rib and one in his left thigh. He seemed to make a good recovery from the chest wound but not from the leg wound, which had to be operated on to remove a bullet which had lodged in his abdomen. He lapsed into unconsciousness and died.

George Hobbs was now accused of the murder of his father and was sent to trial. The jury found him guilty of murder taking only half an hour to deliberate. He was sentenced to die on the gallows and he was sent to Derby Gaol. A petition was raised asking for leniency which went to the

Home Secretary. On 20th December, 1901 his sentence was commuted to imprisonment for life. Life meant life in those days. One wonders if this had happened today he might have been committed to Broadmoor.

Ilkeston parracide
Wrongly named by a newspaper, it should have been written 'Parricide', an old now disused term for Patricide. The former is likely to be a corruption of the latter.

George Smith lived in Bath Street, Ilkeston and worked as a twist hand at a local lace mill. He shared the house with his father Joseph who was a cordwainer (shoemaker) and owned some property in the town. Ilkeston was very much a lace town, an overflow, as was Long Eaton, from Nottingham, the centre of the industry. There is very little left of these mills today. At twenty years of age, George had a free and easy existence founded on alcohol, mixing with prostitutes and visiting 'low theatres'.

A local girl, Emma Eyre had given birth to an illegitimate child and she named George as the father. Both father and son would not entertain this. A gallon of beer was offered to his friends in return for visiting Emma but her mother would not let them near to her daughter. On returning to George they advised him not to spend a shilling on the unseen baby. George decided that if he were to live in France he would escape any payments he might have to find to support the baby. He spent the next few hours carousing with his friends paying for a gallon of beer for their consumption. As he sobered up, the idea of living in France seemed less attractive so he moved to Belton near Shepshed, Leicestershire. A few days later George reappeared in Ilkeston where he stole his father's bank book. He took this to Nottingham where his father's bank was and he tried to draw £14 in cash. The bank clerk refused to pay the money to George without a letter authorising the withdrawal. Whilst there, he bought a pistol with powder and caps.

On his return to Ilkeston, he bought a pennyworth of shot for use with his pistol. He then went on a drinking bout and was seduced by a young woman. He then visited his home to find his father lying asleep on a sofa. George went to the bottom of the garden and prepared his pistol for use. He then went into the house to shoot his father but he had meanwhile left the premises. Later George visited the house again to find that his father had not returned so he hid the pistol in a drawer. Before returning to the house yet again, George imbibed a good deal of alcohol. He was by now very drunk. On his third visit, George found his father sitting near to the fire with his head in his hands. An argument started and the father ordered his son out of the house and told him never to return. George recovered the pistol from the drawer and shot his father dead. It was All Fools Day, 1861!

It would appear that George made no attempt to flee the scene of his crime. The Police arrived and arrested him. His trial took place at the Derby Assizes where he was found guilty and he was sentenced to death. He was hanged on 16th August, 1861 before a large crowd of spectators, many having come to town by trains laid on specially for the event. Many of them from the coal mining areas nearby, some having walked great distances.

Matricide

Mary Fallon of Chesterfield

Matricide, the killing of one's mother, is very rare in Britain. Throughout the twentieth century there were only seven men prosecuted and found guilty of this crime and two of these were in Derbyshire. Henry Dye of Chesterfield was delivering newspapers on 6th August, 1907 and one of his clients lived at 3, Spa Street. On arrival at this address, Henry noticed that the front door was open. Out of curiosity, he looked into the house to find a dead woman lying on the floor. It was the body of Mary Fallon, aged fifty-one years. There had been some conflict in the room as indicated by the amount of debris. Mary was disabled and relied on a crutch for getting about. This together with some furniture, glass and crockery were all smashed to pieces. The bloodied crutch and a chair leg lay by the body. Henry fled the scene and returned with P.C. Sykes. It was obviously the scene of a murder. A search led Sykes to a bedroom where he found John Silk asleep in bed. His father was his mother's first husband hence the name. He was wearing a blood stained shirt and trousers and his hands were covered in blood. He was the twenty-nine years old son of the woman downstairs.

P.C. Sykes woke the man who showed genuine concern and distress when told of what had happened to his mother. However, the policeman arrested him on suspicion of being responsible for a murder. The two men went downstairs where Silk tried to wash his hands at the sink which was prevented by Sykes. The Police surgeon arrived quickly and he was able to confirm that the murder had taken place the night before. An external examination revealed that she had suffered serious injuries to her head, throat and face and was badly bruised. Her hair was soaked in blood. Later on the same day, a post mortem examination revealed serious damage to the lungs due to her ribs having been broken, as if she had been stamped on.

On the previous day the suspect had gone to work as normal returning to his home at 1.00 pm. He changed his clothes, and visited a local public house. In a drunken state, he revisited his home several times throughout the afternoon and evening. A next door neighbour had heard Silk arguing with his mother. Some time later, she witnessed Silk's mother handing a bottle to her son asking him to buy some whisky. He broke the bottle and threw fragments of glass into his mother's face. He departed from the house with two friends in tow and they all entered a public house where a dispute occurred with a young couple. The landlord evicted them all. Silk then attempted to continue his dispute with the man from the public house. The young couple left the scene to the cry from Silk, 'By Christ, There'll be a murder in Spa Lane tonight'. His friends tried to quieten him down but he would have none of it. He shouted again, 'It will be our old girl!' Events showed that this was a serious threat and not just the ramblings of a drunkard.

Once at home, he found his mother with Thomas Meakin, a lodger. Silk started an argument about the gas light not being adequate enough to see by. He tried to turn the flame up and his mother told him to leave it alone. Silk responded by hitting his mother on each side of her head with his open hand. He punched her again and as she fell the table tipped over and the gas light was extinguished. Silk carried on beating his mother in the darkness and the lodger heard the old lady cry, 'Mercy'.

Thomas fled the house and found Police Sergeant Prince who advised him to ignore what was after all a drunken brawl. When Thomas returned to the house all was dark and quiet. The door was locked from the inside and he had to spend the night elsewhere. Neighbours told of a disturbance later in the night when an argument started with the sound of a struggle. Silk was arrested for the murder of his mother. His past life came under scrutiny. He had served in the 5th Irish Lancers for eight years, leaving in 1903 honourably discharged and possibly due to illness. When he served in India, he had contracted enteritis which laid him low for many months. He fought in the Boer War in South Africa where he suffered from an unspecified fever but it had been severe enough for him to drop from thirteen stones in weight to seven. By the time he left the army his mother had separated from her third husband. John Silk went to live with his mother to whom he gave a large proportion of his wages. They seemed to live together amicably. Two near relatives told the court that John was addicted to drink and was showing increased violence towards his mother. He was known to have run through the streets of Chesterfield, shouting in the belief that he was still fighting the Boers. It also came to light that his mother was also addicted to drink which made her aggressive. This made for a disastrous partnership which ended in her being murdered by her own son. Mary had been seen drunk on the night of her death. A plea was made to the effect that the illnesses he had suffered whilst abroad when considered together with his previous good conduct made him, in Silk's opinion, a 'very good lad'.

The inquest was held at Spital Cemetery. Silk appeared in the dock at the next assizes. The defence pleaded that Silk was mentally unsound and that any penalty should be for manslaughter and not murder. Expert witnesses were not called to support the plea that Silk's behaviour had worsened after his discharge from the army and that his troubles lay with his disturbed mental state. After retiring for only fifteen minutes, the Jury returned a verdict of guilty of murder.

On Friday, 29th December, 1905 he was executed at Derby Gaol. He swore that he would die the death of a brave man, four journalists who were in attendance confirmed that he did so.

Ada Knighton of Ilkeston

Ada Knighton lived at 1, Bethel Street, Ilkeston which she shared with her husband George, son William, and a daughter Doris Ivy and her son Reginald. Their sleeping arrangements were typical of a small terraced house of that time. George was an invalid and slept in the ground floor living room, his wife and daughter, Ada, aged 55, and Doris Ivy, aged 16, slept in the attic, Ada's son William slept in the front bedroom which he shared with Reginald who was a grand-child. This left an empty room.

Doris went to work as usual on the morning of Monday, 7th February, 1927 and returned in the evening. The family ate their evening meal together and as was their custom, Ada and William resorted to the local public house for a drink, something they did often, especially with William being a collier. On their return, Doris went to bed and fell into a deep sleep. Ada stayed downstairs for some time. Ada who occupied a shared bed with Doris started to moan and was restless. This woke Doris who asked her Mother if she was ill. Ada sat up grabbing Doris's arm in an attempt to sit up. It was assumed that Ada was having a fit of coughing which she often had. Doris then saw the outline of a person at the foot of the bed. It was her brother William who asked what was wrong with Ada.

Doris said that she had been like it for a while. William lit a match stick, looked at the clock and left.

At six o'clock in the morning George woke his family as he did every working day. Ada did not respond so Doris walked round the bed to examine her. She lighted a candle and held it near to her mother and saw a pool of blood on the floor. Doris shook her without response and went down stairs to tell her father that her mother was dead and she was going to call a doctor.

William was already at the Police Station telling the constable on duty that he wished to speak to an Inspector. A few minutes later, William was telling the Inspector that he had killed his mother. 'I have done the old woman in. I have cut her throat with a razor. The razor is lying by the side of the bed.'

On 26th February, 1927, William Knighton faced his trial for the murder of Ada Knighton, his mother. William Knighton did not claim to be innocent but entered a plea of insanity. The jury found otherwise and he was sentenced to death by the Judge. An appeal was held using the argument that Knighton had admitted his offence to the police soon after the murder and had shown no emotion. He had shown nothing but respect towards his mother and had made no attempt at escaping from custody. The Judge referred the matter to the Home Secretary. The latter cancelled the execution and referred the matter to the Court of Appeal. In spite of an accusation from Doris that her father was responsible for the murder this second appeal was not accepted. On Wednesday, 25 April, William Knighton was hanged at Nottingham prison.

A Miscellany

Prostitution

Matlock to London

There are very few accounts of a prostitute's life but we do have the story of one which explains how an innocent girl from the provinces was lured into the world's oldest profession in London. This account is from Mayhew's book *London Labour and London's Poor*, 1862.

Joan (an invented name by the author as her real name is unknown), was born in Matlock. Her father was a stone cutter and polisher, one assumes at Matlock Bath where such work was undertaken at this time.

In 1851 Joan and her father read about the Great Exhibition in Hyde Park, London built by Joseph Paxton, head gardener at Chatsworth. Joan expressed a strong desire to see the exhibition. Her father wrote to an aunt in London asking if Joan could stay with her for a week or so to allow her to see both the exhibition and the legendary shops.

On arrival she found that her aunt was ill with a heavy cold. This meant that Joan would not be escorted around London and her father had to stay in Matlock because of his business. Joan was eager to see the sights and was not willing to wait for her aunt to get better. So she set out alone.

One day she got lost in the metropolis and knocked on a door to ask for directions to Bank Place, Kensington. The woman was a 'madam' who employed prostitutes and would not accept Joan's reason for knocking on her door but insisted instead that she was seeking employment. A long conversation with this and another woman was conducted with some intensity, one of the women assured Joan that she had heard of her father and knew her aunt. Joan must have been very naive to believe this. The more senior woman showed Joan to a bed and to 'help' her to sleep gave her a drink of gin laced with a narcotic. Unknown to Joan, she lost her virginity that night. This made Joan a virtual slave to the procuress, alternating between two brothels such that she looked like a fresh face in each.

We know nothing further about Joan, but she no doubt would have died young of a venereal disease.

Alice Newsome

Alice of Bernard Street, Glossop was charged with drunk and disorderly conduct to which she pleaded guilty. Detective Sergeant Scott stated that at about 5.15 on Saturday evening he was on duty on High Street West, Glossop when he saw the defendant drunk with a crowd of children round her. She kept running at the children as if to strike them. D.S. Scott ordered her away but on arrival in Railway Street she carried on behaving as before. He picked her up and she said that, 'She would ------ well locked up'. She was then taken into custody. The Chief Constable reported to the bench that she had been given many opportunities to reform but would not. Sergeant Scott said that she had been cautioned several times by both the Chief Constable and himself. She kept herself by prostitution and mixed with bad characters. Alice cried out, 'No I don't'. The Chief Constable then reported that she was in the Workhouse the week before. She kept company with people older than herself and made no effort to reform. He had taken her to her home one night recently at midnight, having to drive her home away from the company of men, also people had to turn her out from the house as she was so badly behaved. She had been in prison three times.

The Chairman of the court said he was sorry that there had been no improvement in the defendant's conduct, otherwise they would have dealt with her leniently. She was fined 10s and costs and sent to prison for 14 days with hard labour.

Author's footnote: It is obvious that this poor woman was a severe alcoholic with no-one to rely on. Then as now, prostitution was their only means of finding the money for the purchase of alcohol. Men relied on theft. Hard labour meant what it said. The prisoner was subject to supervised duties such as breaking stones for the highway over long hours and in all weathers often until they fell down with exhaustion. It certainly was not an easy option.

The Resurrectionists

Also known as grave robbers, stiff lifters, body snatchers and sack-'em-up men.

During the early to mid nineteenth century there was a constant demand for human corpses for dissection by surgeons when demonstrating the anatomy of humans to medical students. The usual source of such cadavers was met from those who had been hanged. There were never enough such bodies and the surgeons began to rely on corpses stolen from graves. Those who plied this gruesome trade were known as Resurrectionists. They had to move quickly before decomposition set in. Criminals sentenced to death had a horror of anticipating that they might end up under the surgeon's knife. The next of kin to the newly buried were also worried. Layers of straw were placed about the coffin to alert the mourners of any activity and to slow down the digging. A night watchman might be hired by the better off to mount a vigil for a few nights until the corpse was of no use to the surgeons. They usually armed themselves with cudgels to fight off any would be body snatchers. They had to dig down to a recent coffin, break into it using a crowbar from above and drag the corpse out. The clothing or shroud was removed and put back into the coffin. To steal clothing was larceny and was punishable but not apparently the stealing of corpses, although some judges did not subscribe to this latter idea. The whole process took less than an hour using a wooden spade to reduce the noise.

The next of kin had but few means available to them to prevent this from happening. Keeping a vigil by the grave until the body was unusable was a favourite of the less well off. Those who could afford an iron cage (mortsafe) could rest in their beds at nights. These were too costly for the average citizen. There are many to see in Scotland, especially near to Edinburgh.

In Derbyshire, after calling at The Chequers Inn at Froggatt, the body snatchers took their victims to Padley Woods where cadavers were laid

Chequers Inn, Froggat

on the ground until skeletal when the bones were sold to doctors.

On one occasion a party of three men pulled up in a horse and trap at The Chequers, two of the men went into the inn for a drink, leaving an old lady's body in the trap. She appeared to have dozed off to sleep when the landlord came out of the inn to engage her in conversation. As it appeared that she was not responding he shook her gently where upon she slumped forward and her bonnet fell off. To the landlord's horror she was a corpse. On another occasion, some men unloaded a lifeless passenger from a cart whilst its minders were enjoying a drink in the inn. The corpse was replaced by one of their number adopting the pose of the cadaver. On resuming their journey, the corpse dropped his arm against one of the men who recoiled and shouted that the hand was warm. The response was, 'Yes, and so would you be if you'd have been where I have'. The cargo was abandoned and the men took off at high speed!

The famous Burke and Hare partnership in Edinburgh took the practice too far. They started murdering their victims and selling them on for dissection. Was it worth their while? At £2 to £20 per cadaver, it could provide a good living in the early 1800s.

This bonanza came to an end when the Anatomy Act was passed in 1832 which allowed for human corpses to be used for scientific purposes subject to the agreement of their next of kin and a stringent code of practice.

In the churchyard at High Bradfield there is a Watch House to allow interested parties to keep a vigil for body snatchers.

The Parish Register at the village of Hope records the activities of two body snatchings:

> 16th October, 1831: William Radwell aged 28. Body stolen during the night following burial.
> 2nd October, 1834: Benjamin Wrags of Bradwell, aged 21. Body stolen from grave.

The robber was undoubtedly from Sheffield where there was a demand for corpses by the surgeons at the teaching hospital there. The robbers often used a 'Resurrection Cart' for the purpose. We do not have a description for these carts but one can assume that they were built to be quiet on country roads. Villagers would talk of such carts having awoken them in the night.

It was also known that the surgeons encouraged this practice and paid well for a fresh corpse. It was not unknown for them to order corpses by murdering the victim first and then recovering the body later.

There is no record of a surviving mort-safe in the county.

Mortsafes at Logierait, Scotland (Albert and Eileen Henderson)

The subject became the stuff of folk lore with its lurid tales about body snatching.

The Monocled Mutineer

Percy Toplis was born in Whittington, near Chesterfield, in 1896. He started his criminal activities in 1908 when he was sentenced by the Mansfield magistrates to be given six strokes of the 'birch'. He had obtained two suits by false pretences. Three months later he obtained some newspapers by false pretences and was sentenced by the Chesterfield magistrates to a year's probation. In 1912 he was sentenced to two years hard labour for raping a 15 year old girl, he was 16 years of age at the time.

On his release he joined the RAMC (Royal Army Medical Corp) as a Medical Orderly. He was stationed at Torquay until 15th June when he was sent to Gallipoli to help in the battle that was raging there. After being wounded he had an attack of dysentery. He was sent back to Britain when hostilities ceased. After hospitalisation he was sent to Salonika and Egypt where he contracted malaria. In September, 1917 he was sent back to Britain again and was promptly sent out to India for a short period after which he was sent back to Britain to an RAMC unit in Blackpool. His father died in August of 1918 and Toplis deserted the army.

The First World War ended three months later when Toplis had adopted the role of an army officer. He obtained a watch by using a stolen cheque and was sentenced to hard labour for six months. Then, in 1920, he joined the Royal Army Service Corps (RAMC) whilst still a deserter. He was posted to the well known Bulford Camp in Dorset where along with other soldiers he stole petrol and sold it to local taxi drivers. One of these was found dead at Thruxton Down close to Andover. At near midnight, Toplis was spotted driving a car which had belonged to the dead driver. He was now on the run. The inquest found Toplis guilty of murder in his absence.

He spent two weeks in London masquerading as an army officer with the rank of captain. He disported a monocle to add to his disguise. The hunt was however heating up and he fled to the north of Scotland. He found a cottage which was used as a small hunting lodge at the Well of Lecht, Moray A game keeper spotted smoke coming from one of the chimneys and with the local constable went to investigate. Toplis met the two men and he then shot them with an officer issue Webley Mark VI revolver. Both were wounded but not seriously. To add insult to injury Toplis escaped on the policeman's bicycle. Calling at Edinburgh he made his way across country to Penrith

The Monocled Mutineer in a Captain's Uniform (Penrith Museum)

The Monocled Mutineer's Monocle (Penrith and Eden Museum, Dr Chapman)

where he presented himself, in a private's uniform, to the Border Regiment at Carlisle Castle where he was given aid. It would appear that the army were not on an alert for him.

On 6th June, 1920, whilst walking on the Penrith to Carlisle road, he was accosted by a policeman at Low Hesketh. Topliss was changing from his army uniform into civilian clothes. The constable approached him due to his strange behaviour whereupon Toplis produced his revolver, which frightened the policeman who promptly contacted his office in Penrith. The policeman along with two armed officers set off in a commandeered car and sped to the site. They were accompanied by the Chief Constable's son on a motorcycle complete with a gun. On reaching Plumpton they created an ambush in a barn near to the village church.

Toplis was not aware of this manoeuvre and continued on his way. The most senior of the policemen, Inspector Richie, confronted Toplis who fled firing his gun as he went. The armed officers promptly shot Toplis in the chest and he collapsed into the inspector's arms where he died.

The inquest found that the policeman who shot Toplis was justified in doing so with a verdict of 'justifiable homicide'. He was buried in July 1920 in the Beacon Edge Cemetery at Penrith. It was a pauper's funeral and he was 23 years of age. His full name was Percy Francis Toplis and he masqueraded as Captain Percy Toplis DCM.

The monocle and the revolver are on display in Penrith Museum (Middlegate, Penrith, CA11 7PT Tel: 01768 867466). Plumpton is approximately five miles north of Penrith on the original A6 road. The farm where Toplis hid can still be seen and is known as Romanway Farm.

A legend about Toplis claimed that he took a leading part in a mutiny at Etaples, south of Boulogne, France in 1917. This inspired a book by two journalists William Allison and John Fairley called *The Monocled Mutineer*. This was used as the basis for a four part serial by BBC Television and a play by Alan Bleasdale. Historians of the First World War assert that no such mutiny occurred.

Poaching

Poaching was a source of food for the poor. They argued that wild animals were a gift from God, the land owners looked upon the wild livestock on their land as their own personal property. The punishment for poaching was severe, including hanging. Had the squirearchy had any compassion for the poor, they could have avoided poaching by providing food for the would be poacher, who often had no choice but to steal their prey in order to avoid starvation.

Hung for a sheep

The full version of this well known phrase is: 'It is better to be hanged for a sheep than a lamb'. The poacher could feed his family for longer on a sheep before he died on the scaffold.

Sheep were a valuable commodity and for many years their fleeces were sold to France and Belgium, where they commanded a good price. Sheep are an easy prey for poachers and sheep stealing is still prevalent in the county.

In the 1840s, Josiah Slack stole a sheep and was arrested for so doing. He did not hang as was the custom but instead he was sentenced to transportation to Australia for life. He languished in Derby prison for a while before being sent on to a prison hulk on the Thames at London. The conditions on these hulks were appalling by any standard with poor food, basic sanitation and the prisoners held in shackles with very little exercise. Fever killed many of them.

Whilst in the hulk, Josiah succumbed to a fever and was seriously ill for many weeks. The authorities gave him a reprieve and he was released under licence on condition that he stay away from his family and home village of Middleton-by-Wirksworth. As a consequence he settled in Great Longstone where he became a railway labourer. At the end of his working life he was sent to the workhouse in Bakewell where he died in his seventies.

At these times transportation was a sentence used rather than hanging as the government was eager to colonise Australia, particularly Sydney.

Sheep stealing

John Marshall kept sheep in an enclosure near to Youlgreave a little distance from his home at Greenfield. As the enclosure was distant from his home, Marshall kept a close eye on it and visited it as often as he could. One Saturday morning in December he counted his sheep to find that a wether (castrated male sheep) was missing and by his calculation this must have occurred on the night of the day before.

He called on his neighbour, John Coats, and they planned to track the thief down together. There was no recourse to the police as they did not exist in 1693. They set out, as they had done before, by searching likely locations for concealing a sheep, hoping that they would catch the thief. They had to move quickly before the mutton was consumed and the fleece and bones were buried.

Calls on local farmers drew a blank. Time was running out so they added a farm hand to make three searches. By late on Monday night they had arrived at Alport, a hamlet nearby.

Robert Tompson with his sister Elizabeth were enjoying the warmth of their fire. Their hunger had been satisfied having consumed more meat over three days than they would have had over two months ordinarily. They had laid by some meat for the next few days.

A knock on the door roused them and then a voice shouted 'Open up!' Robert and Elizabeth were numb with fear. The knocking intensified accompanied with shouts and kicks at the door. As it opened Marshall and Coates strode in noticing that a cloth was draped over a stool. Marshall took the cloth off the stool and there was the mutton.

Coates enquired how they had come by the mutton to which Elizabeth answered, 'I bought it at market in Bakewell this morning, a hind quarter and a shoulder of mutton'. The two farmers knew that this was the oldest excuse given under such circumstances. Robert was rigid with fear for he knew the price he would have to pay for stealing a sheep. Marshall referred to Tompson that the latter had a brother nearby. Robert and his sister nodded. They were told to stay where they were whilst Marshall and Coates opened the door and stepped out. Robert and Elizabeth followed them and stood in the doorway looking out to William Tompson's house. The door was open and Marshall and Coates walked in. A few seconds later the third man came in and led them to the rear of the house. Here they found a black pot with mutton suet in it, newly thrown from the window and a second pot lying in the snow.

The next day they were brought before the local justice, Mr William Eyre; he had to listen to two different versions of the story. Robert stated that he had given five shillings to his sister to buy meat at Bakewell and Elizabeth insisted that she had bought a hind quarter and shoulder of mutton from a butcher in Bakewell. Eyre asked for the name of the butcher with a description of how he looked. Elizabeth could not respond to these questions. They were looking guilty by now as it became obvious that the mutton was stolen. It was also unlikely that she would have bought such a quantity of meat and her brother would not have been able to pay five shillings, which represented two or three weeks wages. Eyre became sympathetic towards the defendants but Elizabeth spoiled it by asking if she could alter her statement. The clerk wrote:

'Upon setting down her examination she denies that she threw it out, but that a dog got to it, and that was the occasion of its falling out of the window.' (verbatim from the clerk's register)

The excuses of the four perpetrators fell apart. They knew that it was unlikely that they had bought a large quantity of meat from an unknown

A Miscellany 109

butcher. They were sent to the Assize Court from where they were sent to the hangman for him to do his duty.

Hanged for sheep was not an idle threat in those days of 1693.

Hung Twice

William Collier of Whiston, Staffordshire – this crime was not in Derbyshire but close to Ashbourne and included because of his bizarre punishment – was 35 years of age and had five children to feed. He killed the son of the local landowner Thomas Smith, Lord of the Manor of Whiston Eaves, whose body was found in a wood at Whiston Farm, Kingsley. One can assume that Collier was caught poaching by Smith.

On 6th July 1866, the day after the crime took place, Collier was before the judge charged with wilful murder. The jury found him guilty with a plea for clemency citing his previous good record and his large family in mitigation. The judge was not sympathetic and he sentenced Collier to death by hanging.

A month later on the 7th August, Collier stood on the scaffold watched by a crowd of onlookers. He was positioned on the trap, the hood and noose were placed over his head and the lever pulled. The rope slipped from the overhead beam and this, with Collier vanished through the open trap. The executioner along with two police officers recovered Collier and took him back to the gallows. The executioner apologised to Collier and asked him to wait! The rope was retackled and the lever was pulled for the second time. The victim hanged this time after having to wait six minutes between attempts.

Sheep stealing at Calow

They did not all hang for stealing a sheep. In March, 1834 George Kinder, aged nineteen, was charged with feloniously stealing five ewes at Calow near Chesterfield, the property of German Dean. German was a fairly common male first name at that time. On 12th January, he had 26 ewes and after relocating them in another field found five were missing. There were marks made by the boots of two men leading away from the field. They traced the sheep to Ashbourne where they were found in the possession of a Mr Etches, a butcher in the same town. A witness had seen Kinder sell the sheep to the butcher.

Kinder was arrested. He told the court that he was assisted by a man named Ford, he of the second set of boot prints. They had arranged to meet at the Blue Bell Inn in the town to divide the money between them. After three days in custody Ford was released without charge as there was not enough evidence with which to convict him. Kinder was sent for transportation for life.

Bestiality
A crime associated with animals which attracted stiff sentences and controversy.

In 1833, John Leedham was a gentle and ignorant soul aged twenty years. His offence was bestiality, a crime that filled most people with revulsion. He was a native of Yeldersley, a village South of Ashbourne. His father was a labourer and he was only eight years old when his mother died. When he became eighteen years of age he went to London. The capital was not to his taste so he returned to his native village. In February, 1833 he was charged with the crime which was to cost him his life.

He was tried and sentenced to death. This verdict caused an uproar in the local paper, the *Derby Mercury*. They compared the sentencing of Leedham with another who had committed the same offence in Northampton, where the Judge, Derbyshire's own Lord Chief Justice Sir Thomas Denman, had committed the convict to transportation for life. The general public were uneasy about the sentence and this disquiet caused the case to be summed up again by the *Derby Mercury*: 'Mr Justice Bosanquest (the presiding Judge) has thought proper, on the same circuit, at Derby, to execute a sentence of death pronounced by him on John Leedham! The wretched convict was only twenty years old ... was not known to have committed any former crime ... was a youth of very weak intellect ... in a state of perfect ignorance ... and scarcely capable of distinguishing between right and wrong. Can this be equal justice?'

Petitions to the judge and the Home Office were sent, one including members of the medical profession. These were turned down and John went to the gallows in front of the prison on Vernon Street, Derby. It was Easter Fair and a crowd of 6,000 onlookers had assembled. He went to the gallows in a state of confusion and fear. He was buried in the churchyard at All Saints', Bradley, a village off the Ashbourne to Belper road. There is no evidence of a stone to remember him by.

Pressing to death
This is one penalty which causes disbelief that anyone, even in a barbaric age, would pronounce this sentence. It was used when the prisoner refused to plead. The poor woman was a mute!

She was warned three times of the consequences of not responding. She maintained silence (she probably did not know what had been said to her) and was then given a short time for reflection on her position. The penalty known as the 'Judgement of Penance' was announced thus:

'You will be taken back to the prison whence you came to a low dungeon into which no light can enter. That you be laid on your back on the bare floor with a cloth round your loins, but elsewhere naked. That there be set on your body a weight of iron, as great as you can bear – and greater, that you have no sustenance save on the first day three morsels of the coarsest bread, on the second day three draughts of stagnant water from the pool nearest the prison door, on the third day again three morsels of bread as before and such bread and such water alternately from day to day until you die.'

This was the last time this penalty was carried out. In retrospect it all seemed to be pointless and carried out with gratuitous cruelty and on someone who could neither hear nor speak.

Arson

In July of 1817 four men were convicted of arson. They were John Brown, Thomas Jackson, George Booth and John King, all being charged for setting fire to certain hay and corn stacks, the property of Winfield Halton Esquire of South Wingfield. The four arsonists were kept in jail awaiting a final verdict. Some days after their condemnation, they cherished a hope that pardon or at least mitigation of their sentences might be extended to them. Under this impression they persisted in asserting that they 'seemed but little affected by the solemnities by which they were surrounded'.

In the last few minutes of their execution, three of the men took shelter from a shower of rain. 'A heavy shower happening whilst the men were singing the hymn, two of them deliberately retreated to the shelter of an umbrella which was expanded on the drop and a third placed himself under cover of a doorway.'

Mass trespass

In the High Peak of Derbyshire there is a large plateau called Kinder Scout. Today it is a walkers' paradise and the haunt of bird watchers. It averages 2000 feet above sea level and was famous for its grouse, which were seriously nurtured for the Glorious Twelfth (12th August – the start of the shooting season). By 1932, there was much resentment that access was barred to walkers and ramblers who decided to create a mass invasion onto the plateau.

They congregated at Hayfield, a village at the foot of a run off from the plateau. There were about 500 of them and they started to climb the clough that would take them to the summit. The protesters were mostly from the nearby Manchester area but people turned up from Derbyshire, Cheshire and South Yorkshire.

On their way uphill they were confronted by keepers who had prior knowledge of the event and were out in numbers. A brief struggle ensued and the keepers retreated, the ramblers carried on to Ashop Head. They held a meeting before retreating triumphant to Hayfield. However the police blocked their retreat, checked those present and arrested five who were assumed to be leaders to whom they added one more who had been detained earlier.

Hayfield had witnessed activity over the past week and villagers were anxious about the coming events. Members of the British Workers Sports Federation, whilst not having any connection with the Ramblers' Federation were sympathetic with their aims. They distributed handbills among Hayfield's Sunday walkers urging them to 'take action to open the fine country at present denied us'.

In the morning, chalked notices appeared on the roads leading to Hayfield and leaflets were handed out to disembarking passengers at Hayfield train station. These leaflets invited the walkers to assemble at 2.00 pm at the Recreation Ground for a meeting before the trespass. Hayfield Parish Council had held a meeting and had taken steps to stop the ramblers from attending the proposed meeting. The Derbyshire County Police were there in strength and copies of the by-laws had been posted on the Recreation Ground notice board. One of the by-laws stated that such meetings could not be held in the Ground.

The Deputy Chief Constable of Derbyshire along with Superintendents McDonald and Else arrived to ensure that the regulation was carried out. The Clerk of the Parish Council was in attendance to read the by-law in public should the ramblers attempt to make speeches. The ramblers had second thoughts and decided to carry on with their trespass. At 2 o'clock, 400 of them set out to climb Kinder Scout via Kinder Reservoir. On the way they sang the 'Red Flag' and the 'International'.

When they arrived at Nab Brow they could see keepers on the slopes of Sandy Heys on the other side of William Clough. The men advanced onwards, the women were kept behind and dropped down to the stream and started to climb up the other side. The men confronted the keepers and there was a brief discussion followed by a fight. There were eight keepers against more than forty ramblers. The keepers fought with sticks, the ramblers using their bare hands. Two keepers were disarmed and their sticks were used against them. Some ramblers took their trouser belts off and used them and one person or more was struck by a stone.

There were no serious injuries apart from a keeper who was knocked unconscious and suffered a damaged ankle. He was helped back to Hayfield and taken by car to Stockport Infirmary. After being treated he was fit to go home on the same evening.

The trespassers continued over Kinder Scout passing on the way a Police Inspector who was escorting a man to Hayfield Police Station. They then turned to Ashop Head, the summit of a public foot path that connected Hayfield with the Snake Inn. A halt was made for tea whereupon a contingent of 30 people joined them from Sheffield, who had watched the fight from a distance. They agreed to clear all the litter they had made and a hat was passed round for collecting money to help defend those who had been arrested.

They all walked back to Hayfield, on the way encountering the police again. One of the police tried to detain one of the ramblers, who promptly massed around and frightened off the policeman. On arrival in Hayfield they were met by a Police Inspector in a small car. He suggested that the 200 remaining ramblers form a column and march into the village. They were happy with what they had achieved but trouble was awaiting them. On arrival in Hayfield they were met by police officers and a keeper who searched the column, taking five ramblers and detaining them in the police station.

The next day, the ramblers were taken to New Mills Police Court where they were charged with unlawful assembly and breach of the peace. They pleaded not guilty and were transferred to Derby Assizes. They were found guilty and were sent to prison from two to six months.

The actions of these ramblers led to the access rights we enjoy today. There are several Acts of Parliament that ensure our right to roam and many other acts covering the countryside, the most important one being the National Parks and Access to the Countryside Act. The benefits of climbing on to a plateau such as Kinder Scout after a bruising week in a factory are boundless. It frees the spirit.

In 2002, the 11th Duke of Devonshire publicly apologised on the 70th anniversary celebration event of the Kinder Trespass at Bowden Bridge. He also apologised for his grandfather's and other land owners' 'great wrong' of 1932.

On 18th April, 2007, the seventy fifth anniversary of the trespass was celebrated by many. Chief amongst the visitors were Tom Stephenson and

Benny Rothman (one of those sent to prison) who planned and led the trespass on 25th April, 1932.

One word of warning – the weather on this plateau is fickle. It can change suddenly from bright warm sunshine to bitter cold winds often presaging snow.

Bigamy

Eleven wives

Samuel Charles Joseph Woodward (aka James Walker, William Ford et. al.), a native of Derby born circa 1853, committed bigamy on an industrial scale.

Wife 1 – His first marriage on 21st November, 1875 was held at Saint Peter's Church in Derby. We only know her maiden name as being Lawrence. A year later he went into business in the town as an accountant and agent and on 5th January, 1887 he fled with the money he had taken. A warrant for his arrest was issued but withdrawn when an anonymous donor repaid it in full. He was wanted again for embezzlement in Wantage, Oxfordshire.

Wife 2 – In 1892, he was in Newcastle on Tyne where he married again and ended up drugging his new wife before he left her. During 1895-7 he lived in Surrey where he worked for a company of Solicitors absconding with £520 of their money. This was on 24th November, 1897. He was next found in Sunderland under the name of William Ford but he absconded to avoid the law.

Wife 3 – Having renamed himself as William Herbert de Ford he married a woman from Sunderland on 15th January, giving his address as Leamington, Ontario, Canada. He left her when in Edinburgh two days later.

Wife 4 – On 23rd February, 1898 he married a Maggie Clark in Carlisle.

Wife 5 – In the same year he was in Lancaster where he married again, only one month after wife 4.

Wife 6 – On 12th January, 1899 he married a woman from Wolverhampton. In the following year he was in Stratford, Essex working as a solicitor's clerk under the name of Wilson. He departed from them carrying £80 of their cash.

Wife 7 – Again, he was employed as a solicitor's clerk in Cardiff under the name of Horatio Lawrence. He borrowed money from one of the partners 'to attend his father's funeral'. They did not hear from him again. Whilst in Cardiff he married yet again and she was left behind when he absconded. We next find him in Colchester where in May he joined another

A Miscellany

solicitor as a clerk, his name this time being Millard. At this month end he vanished complete with £47 in cash and carrying the keys of the cash box. In June, 1901, he surfaced in the Strand, London working as a solicitor's clerk whom he left two months later carrying £200 and the key to the safe. In 1906, with Maggie Clark in tow they arrived in Penrith which town he left carrying some deeds. They then lived in Bradford and Wolverhampton amongst many other towns. By August, 1907 he had left Maggie.

Wife 8 – He then met and married Fanny Henderson Davis at Huddersfield.

Wife 9 – Changing his name yet again, this time to Thomas Davis, he married again at Warwick. His new wife was persuaded to sell her business whilst they were planning to go to the United States of America together. He abandoned her carrying her jewellery.

Wife 10 – 3rd March 1908 and he married a woman from Gloucester and promptly stole her money.

Wife 11 – A month later he married a lady at Bristol.

He appeared in court at Huddersfield under the name of James Walker, described as a confectioner and doctor. The court chose the marriage at Derby as his first wife apparently had two children. The court were told that there had been eleven marriages and there were seven warrants outstanding in his name covering embezzlement, larceny and forgery. It would appear that he was let off as there is no account of his sentence.

Foot note: it was likely that he did go to the United States of America. The police there found no evidence of his activities. There might be more wives?

Wife selling
Is this illegal? It was common practise in Derbyshire many years ago and such events went unnoticed. One assumes that the woman agreed to this arrangement beforehand? Had she married the second man it would have been bigamy, subject to the law. It was required of the first man to agree a price or goods in lieu of or additional to money with the woman. Many wives were taken to market in this manner to show that there were available for sale. The woman would be paraded round the market with the husband extolling her virtues, or he might pay the town crier to do this for him. When this was in progress the wife would be tethered by a halter to her neck to allow her husband to parade her such that onlookers could recognise what was happening. She would then be auctioned to the highest bidder.

The only instances available were:
> On market day at Derby on 5 December, 1772, Thomas Bott sold his wife for 18d in cash to a man from Langley Common. The sale was ratified in a local hostelry.
> Some years later a man sold his wife at Chesterfield Market in exchange for a sheep dog and a bale of hay.
> 18d was considered a fair and proper price to pay at the time.
> In Thomas Hardy's book *The Mayor of Casterbridge* a man sells his wife to a sailor. The book was published in 1886.

Gambling

Twelve young men at Holbrook near Belper decided that they would enjoy a game of cards played for money. This was on Sunday, 16th August, 1896 when such pastimes were illegal, especially on a Sunday thus adding to their guilt.

They chose a field called Stonewalls which was also known as Dumble Field. They felt that the location was unsuitable so they moved to another field known as Rowlands Field where the gaming recommenced. They placed a young man, Charles Fletcher to keep watch and to warn of the arrival of the police. The eleven carried on gambling playing a game called 'Banker' one of them losing a week's wages very early.

Sergeant Turner and P.C. Arnold arrived and arrested them all but later Fletcher was not charged. The remainder were brought before the Belper Magistrates. They pleaded not guilty using the argument that they were playing on private property and that there had been no offence. The police argued that the playing had moved on to a footpath and therefore an offence had been committed.

The Magistrates would have none of this and found them all guilty. The oldest being the ringleader was fined 15 shillings and 9 pence being a week's wages, the remainder were fined 10 shillings and 9 pence, or in default 15 and 7 days in jail respectively.

Road Traffic Offences

There is nothing new!

James Sutton appeared under summons against him for riding without reins on the highway at Hadfield near Glossop. P.C. Pegg had cautioned Sutton on a previous occasion for this misdemeanour. He was fined 1 shilling and costs and in default 14 days in the House of Correction. It is not recorded which he chose.

James Booth was charged by P.C. MacEare with leaving his cart standing between High Street and Victoria Street, Glossop for 55 minutes. He was fine 5 shillings and costs and in default one month in prison.

A load of timber in Glossop
Thomas Sidebottom and George Clarke, both carters, were charged with being drunk and incapable when in charge of a laden cart. Superintendent Williams had been informed that there were two carts laden with timber with two drunkards in charge. A 'medical man' reported that one of the men was unfit to be moved. He was fined 5 shillings as a warning to others!

Witchcraft
Witchcraft was rare in the county and there are very few accounts dealing with their prosecution. The well known Witchfinder General, Matthew Hopkins, a shipping clerk, from Grantham, Lincolnshire was busy executing witches in the East of England from 1645-47 but did not reach Derbyshire. The presence of a witch was recorded in Bakewell in 1608. A lodging house keeper and milliner, Mrs Stafford, was indicted for practicing witchcraft.

A Scotsman whilst lodging at her premises awoke in the night to see a light beaming from a joint in the floorboards. He looked through the joint and witnessed Mrs Stafford with another women who was dressed for travelling. Mrs Stafford pronounced the words, 'Over thick, over thin. Now Devil, to the cellar in Lunnun'. This last word was slang for London. The room became dark and he sensed that the two women had left. Not knowing what to do, he used the same incantation but mixed the words, 'Through thick, through thin, Now, devil, to the cellar in Lunnun'. He was transported by a wind which took him to London where he landed in a poorly lit cellar. The two women were already there and were tying parcels of silk. The Scotsman realised that they were witches and that the goods were stolen. They offered him wine which he drank and he fell into a deep sleep. He awoke to find himself alone in the cellar, the witches having fled.

The hapless Scotsman was arrested by a watchman and was arraigned before a Magistrate. He was charged with being in an empty house with felonious intent. The Magistrate asked why he was only partially dressed and he explained that the missing items were still in Bakewell. He then told of his strange adventure. The Magistrate noted that this was an example of Witchcraft. The statements were sent to Derbyshire where Mrs Stafford and her accomplice were tried and sentenced to death. There was however, an alternative story. The Scotsman when staying at the lodging house found himself owing back rent. As a consequence Mrs Stafford evicted him keeping some of his clothes as a surety for his paying the outstanding money. The Scotsman made for London where he formulated his revenge. He found an empty cellar where he removed most of his clothes and then sent for a watchman. He was taken before a Magistrate to whom he related his second adventure. There is no record that the women were tried or of their fate.

In 1608, one of the assizes was held at Chesterfield during an outbreak of the plague in Derby. Four years later, the famous witch trials of Pendle Hill, Lancashire were held.

The Witch Act of 1712 was last used in 1944 at no less a court that the Old Bailey. A spiritualist was tried for forecasting accurately the future conduct of World War II.

Sources and acknowledgements

The material for this book is from the author's collection unless otherwise stated. One must be mindful that each of the more serious crimes are well covered from a variety of sources, most claiming copyright although more than seventy years have elapsed since these events occurred.

Newspapers and Newsletters
Bristol Mercury and Daily Post
Derbyshire Family History Society Newsletter
Derby and Chesterfield Reporter
Derby Mercury
Heanor Observer
Holbrooke Village Magazine
Glossop Dale Chronicle
Lloyds Weekly Newspaper
Macclesfield Courier
Macclesfield Mercury
Mansfield and North Nottinghamshire Advertiser
Matlock Mercury
Peak Advertiser (Julie Bunting)
Rome News Tribune

Books
Annals of Crime in the East Midland Circuit and the Biographies of noted Criminals of Nottinghamshire, Derbyshire, Lincolnshire, and Leicestershire, 1862.
Confessions of Percival Cooke and James Tomlinson. Nottingham n.d.
Derbyshire Graves. Peter Naylor. Spondon. 1992
From the Cradle to the Grave. Elizabeth Eisenberg Derby. 1992
Hanged for a Sheep. E. G. Power. Cromford. 1981
History of the Matlocks. Peter Naylor. Ashbourne. 2003
London Labour and the London Poor. Henry Mayhew. 1862
Illustrated History of Belper and its Environs. Ed. Peter Naylor. Belper. 2000
May the Lord have Mercy on your Soul P. Taylor. Derby. 1989. Ed. Peter Naylor

Rolls of the Derbyshire Eyre. Ed. Aileen Hopkinson for the Derbyshire Records Society. Volume XXVII. Cheterfield.2000.
Spondon a History. S. Watson. Derby. 1989
The Coterol Gang: an anatomy of a band of Fourteenth Century Criminals, with the kind permission of the Oxford University Press and Dr J. G. Bellamy, Carleton University Canada..

Collections
Local Studies at Derby, Glossop, Chesterfield, Matlock
Glossop Heritage Centre.

Websites
http://find.galegroup.com
www.lastminute.com
www.legendarydartmoor.co.uk
www.rotherham.web.co.uk
www.scviencvemuseum.org.uk

The author expresses his gratitude to the following

Kate Lloyd for checking the script and for chauffeuring me.
Robin Hall and Richard Carr for bringing the copy-cat murders to my attention.
Stuart Flint of Wirksworth for items in his family history research.
Robert and Eileen Henderson of Logierait, Perthshire for the photograph of the mortsafe.
Jane Evans of Sigma Press for her guidance and patience as well as her editing skills for which the writer will be eternally grateful.

About the author

Peter Naylor has over twenty books to his name along with several articles in journals and part inputs to other works. He has appeared on Radio Derby many times and has also appeared on a television programmes, acting as the link man on one.

He is married with an adult son. He languished in a sanatorium for two years where he studied all manner of things. During his working life he has been a Police Officer, engineer, technical author, director of two companies, lecturer at Nottingham University and the Workers Education Association and has taught on leisure programmes at several adult colleges from Wiltshire in the south to the Wirral in the north, consultant to five local authorities, is an honorary member of the Peak District Mines Historical Society and was the chairman of a trade association for two years. He has also been a Juryman of the Great Barmote Courts in Derbyshire for 37 years, the oldest surviving leet court in the United Kingdom.

He boasts two degrees, has held a radio amateur call sign, was a parish councillor and school governor.

Peter is also well known dowser having written a best selling book on the subject, now in its seventh reprint.

Also from Sigma Leisure:

Traditional Derbyshire Fare
300 recipes plus the stories and anecdotes behind them
Jill Armitage
Some Derbyshire dishes are well known, like the Bakewell Pudding; many more, including some of the most delectable, are little known outside the places whose name they bear. The recipes are individual, easy, economical, with readily available ingredients, and have a strong regional accent. This is Derbyshire food at its best.
£12.95

Walks in the Ancient Peak District
Robert Harris
A collection of walks visiting the prehistoric monuments and sites of the Peak District. A refreshing insight into the thinking behind the monuments, the rituals and strange behaviour of our ancestors. All the routes are circular, most starting and finishing in a town or village that is easy to locate and convenient to reach by car.
£8.99

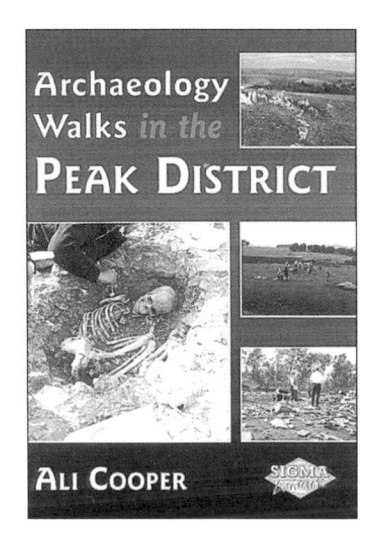

Rocky Rambles in The Peak District
Fred Broadhurst

"The Peak District has a dramatic story to tell and Fred Broadhurst is just the guide we need." – Aubrey Manning, presenter of the BBC TV series 'Earth Story'.

You don't have to be an expert or even an amateur geologist to enjoy these 'rocky rambles'! Where better than in and around the Peak District would you find geology right there beneath your feet - all you need to know is where to look.

The comprehensive glossary of terms, which covers the identification of Peak District Rocks, forms an invaluable supplement and provides 'at a glance' information for the reader.

£8.95

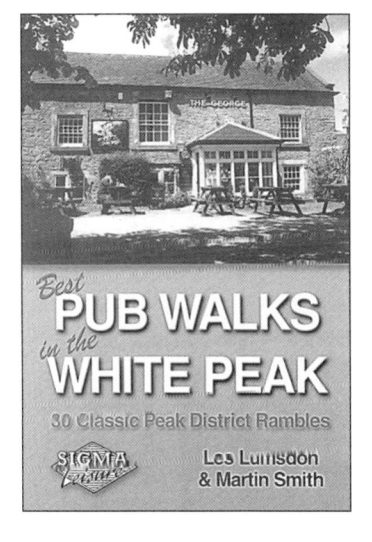

Peak District Walking – On The Level
Norman Buckley

Some folk prefer easy walks, and sometimes there's just not time for an all-day yomp. In either case, this is definitely a book to keep on your bookshelf. Norman Buckley has had considerable success with "On The Level" books for the Lake District and the Yorkshire Dales.

The walks are ideal for family outings and the precise instructions ensure that there's little chance of losing your way. Well-produced maps encourage everybody to try out the walks - all of which are well scattered across the Peak District.

£7.95

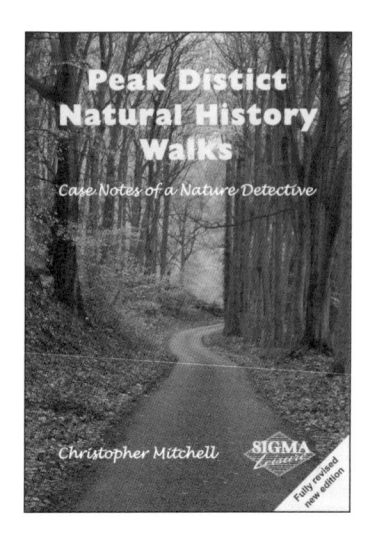

Peak District Walking Natural History Walks
Christopher Mitchell
An updated 2nd Edition with 18 varied walks for all lovers of the great outdoors — and armchair ramblers too! Learn how to be a nature detective, a 'case notes' approach shows you what clues to look for and how to solve them. Detailed maps include animal tracks and signs, landscape features and everything you need for the perfect natural history walk. There are mysteries and puzzles to solve to add more fun for family walks — solutions supplied! Includes follow on material with an extensive Bibliography and 'Taking it Further' sections.
£8.99

Best Tea Shop Walks in the Peak District
Norman and June Buckley
A wonderful collection of easy-going walks that are ideal for families and all those who appreciate fine scenery with a touch of decandence in the shape of an afternoon tea or morning coffee —or both! The 26 walks are spread widely across the Peak District, including Lyme Park, Castleton, Miller's Dale, and The Roaches and — of course — such famous dales as Lathkill and Dovedale. Each walk has a handy summary so that you can choose the walks that are ideally suited to the interests and abilities of your party. The tea shops are just as diverse, ranging from the splendour of Chatsworth House to more basic locations. Each one welcomes ramblers and there is always a good choice of tempting goodies.
£7.95

Derbyshire Walks with Children
William D Parke

There are 24 circular walks, ranging from 1 to 6 miles in length, and each one has been researched and written with children in mind. The directions and background information have been checked and revised as necessary for this updated reprint.

Detailed instructions for parents and an interactive commentary for children mean there's never a dull moment. There are even 'escape routes' to allow families to tailor each walk to suit their own needs, time and energy

"The needs, entertainment and safety of children have been of paramount importance."
– Peak Advertiser
£7.95

All-Terrain Pushchair Walks: The Peak District
Alison Southern

The Peak District, in the heart of the country, has some of England's most picturesque landscapes, from the White Peak in the south with its rocky outcrops and steep hills, to the Dark Peak in the north with peat moss moorland and stunning vistas. This book is for families with all-terrain pushchairs and buggies, and for everyone wishing to avoid as many stiles and obstacles as possible. Includes family-friendly attractions, trees to identify, birds and plants to spot, and lots more to discover. Have fun while you walk enjoying the amazing views, have some healthy exercise and spend time with the family away from the modern world.

£7.95.

Peak District Trigpointing Walks
Hill walking with a point to it!
Keith Stevens & Peter Whittaker

A superb introduction to an intriguing new walking experience: searching out all those elusive Ordnance Survey pillars. Packed with detailed walks to new and interesting Peak District summits, with a wealth of fascinating information on the history of the OS and the art of GPS navigation.

There are 150 Peak District Ordnance Survey pillars — can you find them all? Walk to all the best scenic viewpoints — from the top you can spot all the surrounding pillars. This book shows you how.
£8.95

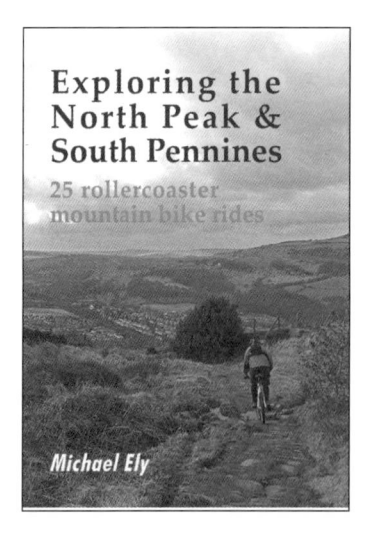

Exploring the North Peak & South Pennines
25 rollercoaster mountain bike rides
Michael Ely

This book will inspire you to pump up the tyres and oil the chain for some excitement, exercise and a feast of rollercoaster riding as you join Michael Ely on some great mountain biking in these Pennine hills. Over 500 miles of riding for the adventurous off-road cyclist that explore the tracks and steep lanes in the Pennine hills. There are twenty-five illustrated rides - with cafe stops half way round - to provide both a challenge and many hours of healthy exercise in classic mountain biking country.
£8.99

Rocky Rambles in The Peak District
Fred Broadhurst

"The Peak District has a dramatic story to tell and Fred Broadhurst is just the guide we need." – Aubrey Manning, presenter of the BBC TV series 'Earth Story'.

You don't have to be an expert or even an amateur geologist to enjoy these 'rocky rambles'! Where better than in and around the Peak District would you find geology right there beneath your feet - all you need to know is where to look.

The comprehensive glossary of terms, which covers the identification of Peak District Rocks, forms an invaluable supplement and provides 'at a glance' information for the reader.

£8.95

Peak District Walking – On The Level
Norman Buckley

Some folk prefer easy walks, and sometimes there's just not time for an all-day yomp. In either case, this is definitely a book to keep on your bookshelf. Norman Buckley has had considerable success with "On The Level" books for the Lake District and the Yorkshire Dales.

The walks are ideal for family outings and the precise instructions ensure that there's little chance of losing your way. Well-produced maps encourage everybody to try out the walks - all of which are well scattered across the Peak District.

£7.95

Beatrix Potter's Derwentwater
Joyce Irene Whalley and Wynne Bartlett

A fascinating look at the beautiful Derwentwater area as Beatrix Potter depicted in her sketches and books. Includes paintings and sketches by Beatrix Potter and photographs both old and new make this an invaluable book for visitors to the Lake District, and all those who know and love Peter Rabbit and his friends.

Detailed routes are included for three walks starting from Keswick so readers can explore the wonderful scenery found in the stories of Benjamin Bunny, Squirrel Nutkin and Mrs Tiggie-winkle.

£9.99

The Charlie Chaplin Walk
Stephen P Smith

Explore the London streets of Charlie Chaplin's childhood in a chronological tour that can be taken on foot or from the comfort of an armchair. This book concentrates on the story of Chaplin's formative years and takes a fresh look at the influence they had upon his films.

For fans of Chaplin, those interested in film history and anybody with an interest of the social history of London's poor of the late Victorian and early Edwardian era.

£9.99

All of our books are all available through booksellers. For a free catalogue, please contact:

SIGMA LEISURE, STOBART HOUSE, PONTYCLERC, PENYBANC ROAD AMMANFORD, CARMARTHENSHIRE SA18 3HP
Tel: 01269 593100   Fax: 01269 596116

info@sigmapress.co.uk   www.sigmapress.co.uk